A BOOKISH ROMANTIC COMEDY

My Turn

FROM THE AUTHOR OF *HER TURN*

ALLISON JONES

Edited By Christie Stratos of Proof Positive
Design and distribution by Bublish, Inc.

ISBN: 978-1-647044-73-2 (paperback)
ISBN: 978-1-647044-72-5 (eBook)

Dedication

To my mother ... thank you for encouraging me to be a writer long before I knew it was my dream. I miss you.

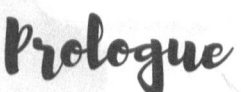

Prologue

Nina

"She looks good. It's an improvement from the caked-on makeup she wore that made her look like a clown. Sad that death improved her looks." Grammy is never one to mince words. We are attending the visitation of her dearly departed "friend," Mildred Conway. The friend is in quotations because Mildred wasn't exactly kindhearted. In fact, she did her best to make sure everyone in town knew that her shit, in fact, didn't stink. The Conway family rules our small West Virginia town with an iron fist. Oh and—wait for it—the town is even named for the family. Conway, West Virginia, is a stifling town full of nothingness. Money talks. Poverty is so loud, it's deafening.

Grammy raised me since my parents both were killed in an automobile accident when I was a baby. I don't remember anything about them, but Grammy makes sure that I never forget them. She filled our small, two-bedroom home with photographs of them. Recipes that she and her daughter, my mother, prepared together have been passed down to me. Grammy is my heart.

My full name is Georgina Marie Bryant. Everyone calls me Nina. Growing up in this rural town, there are no secrets, yet there are. Does that make sense? What I mean is that you can't take a shit without the whole world knowing, but there are things of the dark variety that never seem to surface. No one talks about it. It's just one of the reasons I can't wait to leave this godforsaken town. And I will, because I have a plan.

As we melt into the crowd of people that turned out to pay their respects to Mildred, my eyes meet the one person in town who could literally make my heart stop. Harrison McCall is beautiful. At the ripe age of seventeen, he is already sculpted like an Adonis. Ripped muscles, sandy-brown hair, and the most piercing chocolate eyes I have ever seen. He is perfect.

And totally out of my league.

Why?

Because I'm awkward, gangly, and extremely shy. My jet-black hair is straight and stringy. I usually wear it in a ponytail because I simply can't style it any other way. My facial features are dull. Brown eyes, button nose, and thin lips. Boring. The only thing I have going for me is my height. At 5'7, my long legs make up for my appearance.

Harrison's eyes meet mine and he gives me a wink. Sometimes I wonder if that's a twitch he can't control. He winks at everyone. He's like a wink whore. I roll my eyes. My face reddens. I can't control that—it seems to change color whenever I am in his presence.

We pay our respects to the family, saying socially acceptable things like, "I am so sorry for your loss," "She was such a wonderful person"— you know, the usual. No one would dare utter the truth about the troll. Like, "Sorry about that cold-hearted bitch." Nope, we just smile and dole out the lies as if they were appetizers at a fancy function.

As we make our way through the crowd and out to Grammy's 1965 Ford Rambler, her pride and joy, a voice calls my name. I turn around to find it's Harrison. Gorgeous, unattainable Harrison.

"Nina, hey, wait up!" I stop. He runs toward me. Grammy has already gotten in the car, and she smiles in my direction. I feel my face redden as my throat constricts.

"Umm, yeah." Check out my super-cool lines, ladies and gentlemen. He grins at me with his ridiculously adorable dimples.

"Do you have a date for prom?" He might as well have asked me if I was planning to land on the moon. I stand there like a statue. "Nina, did you hear me?"

"I heard you. No, I-I don't." I don't look at him. If I look at him then my face will redden even more.

"Want to go with me?" His hands are in the pockets of his pressed khakis. He seems nervous.

"Me? You want to go with me? Why?" I tilt my head as I ask, not really wanting to know the answer.

"Why? Because I think it would be fun. Come on. It's senior prom." He says it so nonchalantly. Like it would be normal for the most popular, beautiful boy in our senior class to ask the quirky, quiet girl to prom. Color me confused.

"Umm, sure. I guess that would be fine." I twirl my ponytail while I stare at my feet.

"Gee, don't sound so excited." As I meet his gaze, his face is blanketed in hurt.

"I'm sorry. I'm just surprised you asked me. There are so many other girls prettier than me who you could ask." I flinch at my own admission.

"No other girl is you." He smiles at me and I smile back, surprised. "I'll call you with the details."

"Okay." My heart races as he turns and walks away. The boy of my dreams is taking me to prom. *Prom.* That's the one event I was going to skip. My friends, Cassie and Marley, have dates. I was the lone wolf per usual, but now I can't contain my excitement.

I get into the car to find Grammy grinning. "Do we need to go to the dress shop, Georgina?" She refuses to call me Nina.

"Grammy, that would be too expensive. I can just wear something from the thrift store." Money is tight. I've been saving my earnings from babysitting and working at the town ice-cream shop to go toward my expenses for college, even with my full ride to NYU. Yes, while I am quirky, I am also brilliant. Not to toot my own horn, but my brain is getting me out of this hellhole of a town. Grammy has always encouraged me to follow my dreams and never once has asked me to stay for her sake. I love her for that.

"Nonsense, you need a new dress, new shoes—the works. No granddaughter of mine is wearing someone else's hand-me-downs to an event. We can go shopping tomorrow."

Harrison

My heart races when I spot Nina in the crowd. For months, I have been watching the quiet girl. The girl who sits on the bleachers while the football team practices, not cheering, not even paying attention. She isn't like the others who are just there to watch boys in tight pants. Her nose is in a book. She tries to blend into the metal. To be invisible, but I see her, and I want to get to know her.

I know what you're thinking. I can already hear your criticism. You think I'm just going to use her. Sure, I can get any girl to go out with me. There isn't a shortage of options, but there's something about her. I've been working up the nerve to ask her. While others are doing "promposals," which, for the record, are totally ridiculous, I'm still practicing my spiel. Because I know she's going to be confused. The reality is that I've barely spoken to her. Aside from the casual "hello" or a question about an assignment, there haven't been deep conversations. The nervousness eats at me.

When I see her at the funeral home, I realize that this is my chance. Yes, it's an odd venue, but I'm running out of time. Melanie Hart is expecting me to ask her. After all, we used to date. We were the popular couple, the couple everyone was jealous of, but when I found out she'd slept with several of my teammates, I split from her fast. She still has other ideas.

Nina's eyes sparkle when I ask her. At least they do when she finally makes eye contact. She is stunning. She has no idea how many guys want to ask her out, but she's standoffish. It intimidates a lot of guys.

She doesn't have money like my parents do, but who cares about that? I mean, what difference does it make? My friends say it matters—they only date girls who have as much money as their families have. But I don't know. It seems weird to me to care so much about that. I don't think they'll react to me taking Nina to prom very well, but school's almost over anyway. Whatever.

As her grandma's car drives away, I find myself shrugging off the reaction my family and friends are going to have. All I care about is that Nina said yes.

Nina

Grammy and I step through the door of the only dress shop in town. She's all smiles as we peruse the various frilly dresses. I try not to look at the price tags, knowing that will only embarrass her. A gorgeous pink dress layered in chiffon catches my eye. I'm drawn to it and run my fingers over the fabric.

"Do you want to try that on?" the salesperson asks me.

"Umm, I'm just looking," I whisper.

"Nonsense, she'll try that on, and I think it will be perfect." Grammy grins at me.

I glance at her. Her eyes dance in delight and I smile back. I take the dress into the fitting room, strip off my clothes, and hesitate. I think this is the first piece of clothing I've ever tried on that wasn't from a thrift store. I unzip the back of the dress and step into it, pulling the delicate fabric up my body. As I zip up the back, I feel like I'm in heaven. My hands smooth the front of the dress. The chiffon fabric feels divine and it fits perfectly. It molds to me as if it were custom made by a fancy designer. My euphoria quickly dissipates as I glance at the price tag. I gasp. Two hundred dollars for a dress? I can't even fathom it, so I swallow my disappointment. I glance at myself in the mirror one more time, hoping to burn it into my memory, because that's where it's staying. Taking it off and putting my jean shorts and T-shirt back on, I walk out of the dressing room.

"It didn't fit." I don't look at Grammy.

"Is that so?" Her voice is dripping in sarcasm. She knows me so well. I can't lie around her to save my life.

"I just don't like it as much as I thought." I try to say it with some conviction.

"Well, girl, make up your mind. Do you not like it or does it not fit? Or perhaps you're lying to your elderly grandmother." Oh yes, she is the queen of manipulation with her subtle passive-aggressive taunts.

"It's too expensive." I whisper so the saleslady doesn't hear us.

"Nonsense. I have some money and I want to spend it on my beautiful granddaughter. Let the old lady have some fun." She smiles at me while she holds my face in her hands. "You deserve to have something exquisite for this special night. Please, let me do this."

"Thank you, Grammy. I love you." I smile at her and walk into her warm embrace.

"You're very welcome. Now we need to find some shoes to match. No arguments, you hear?" She uses her stern voice and I simply nod in agreement. I have never won an argument with her in my life, and I am certainly not going to now.

Harrison

I can't believe I'm so nervous. I'm never nervous with girls. As I put on my tux—no jokes, please, my parents force me to wear it to their formal functions—my stomach flutters in a way I'm not used to. In the last few weeks, Nina and I have spent a lot of time on the phone talking. I love how passionate she is about her plans to go to New York and her academic scholarship to NYU. We talk about books, and I even told her how much I love reading, something no one else knows. I could never tell my friends that. They'd label me as a geek, and I'm not. I just like to read. So what? They just don't get it.

We made plans for me to pick her up at seven and head to the country club for dinner, where most of my friends are going. Lost in thought, I almost didn't hear my mother knocking on my door.

"Come in," I say, looking myself over in the mirror.

"Hey, honey! Don't you look handsome. Melanie's here with her parents. We want to get pictures before you go." My mother is dressed in a designer pantsuit, with her perfectly coiffed blond hair.

"I'm not going with Melanie, Mom. I'm taking Nina Bryant. I told you that last week." Does she not remember that? It was a whole discussion.

"Oh sweetie, I thought you were kidding. No, you're going with Melanie. It's a better match." She is completely serious. "Now, let's go downstairs, and honey, please smile. Melanie looks stunning in her dress. You make a gorgeous couple."

She leaves the room without another word. I stare at the open door and start to sweat. Seriously? That's it? This is a nightmare. I pace back and forth in my room. What the hell do I do now? I can't call Nina and tell her what happened. That would be so embarrassing. And I can't tell my parents no. The fact that I can't is even more embarrassing.

I am so fucked.

Okay, I don't have a choice. My parents have made up my mind for me as usual. God, I'm going to seem like such an asshole to Nina. I'll take Melanie to prom—I can't exactly go outside and tell her and her parents to head home, right?—and ghost Nina. Maybe she'll understand in the long run. She can't hate me for doing what my parents tell me ...

It's not just about prom, anyway. I'm an only child; I'm supposed to carry on the family name in business. My life has been planned out already, and Nina isn't part of my parents' plan. She's got to understand that. I really hope she doesn't hate me.

Nina

I'm still waiting. The clock reads 7:45 p.m. and every time I call his cell, it goes to voicemail. My hair is styled in ringlets framing my face. The pink chiffon dress is paired with strappy black heels. Low heels, of course, as I don't want to kill myself before I even get to the prom. My makeup is subtle. I feel beautiful for the first time ever. At least, I did at seven o'clock, when he was supposed to come. Now I think I was right all along. There was no way Harrison really wanted to be with me. I was just a joke.

I pick up my purse and gather my keys. I can't sit in this house one more minute looking at Grammy's sad eyes. It kills me that she went to all this trouble, spent a lot of money, just for me to be stood up.

"I'm going to prom, Grammy." I look at her, and her expression of pity tells me my own face is riddled with emotion. I can't hide anything.

"Are you sure?"

"Yes, I need to find out what happened. I'm not sitting around here like a victim. That's not how you raised me."

She grins at me proudly. "That's my girl. You call me if you need me." She hugs me. "Don't allow anyone else's actions to define you. You are strong, beautiful, smart, and kind. Those traits will carry you far."

I sure hope I can do this.

The short drive feels like it's taking years. When I finally pull into the school parking lot, I pause and take a deep breath. I get out and slam the door, prepping myself for whatever I'm about to find out.

As I walk into the decorated gym, eyes follow me. Whispers float around me. Then I see them. Melanie and Harrison dancing together. Melanie, Harrison's popular, pretty ex. Her hands are wrapped around his neck. How stupid and gullible I was to believe that he would want someone like me. As if he feels my presence, our eyes meet. He untangles himself from Melanie and comes toward me. Temporarily paralyzed, I simply stand in place. Melanie looks pissed.

"Nina, I am so sorry. I can explain. I wanted to take you, but then my parents insisted I had to take Melanie. I didn't even know until she showed up at my house tonight. It isn't what I wanted." His face is full of sorrow and regret, but I'm not buying it.

I dig deep for my inner bitch because my soft, naïve nature isn't going to help in this situation. He deserves anything I say to him.

"That's okay, Harrison. I totally understand," I say sarcastically, smirking. "I guess you would have to have balls to stand up to your parents. Sounds like they run your life. It's a shame—I thought you were such a big deal. Guess not. Later, and good luck with your dismal existence."

His face falls, shoulders slouch, and at that moment, I can't wait to leave this town. I turn on my brand-new heels to exit the building. Head held high, I salute them with my middle finger and don't look back. I never will.

I get to the parking lot. My hands are shaking. I can't believe I just stood up for myself. It was freeing and terrifying. Tears streaming down my face, I hear voices screaming my name. I look up and my two best friends, Cassie and Marley, are running toward me. Without a word, they hug me tight. As they pull away, both grab my hands.

"Are you alright?" Cassie asks. Her face laced with concern. Both of my friends are kind and beautiful. We have been best friends since preschool, and I know they always have my back.

"What a dick!" Marley blurts. She's the badass of our trio.

I giggle through the tears.

"I'm not okay, but I will be. Go back to your dates. I'm going home."

"We could do a girls' night at my house! Come on. Prom is lame and so are our dates," Cassie says.

They went with the Anderson twins, who are big partiers. They are probably high as a kite by now.

"Guys, I appreciate your support. Really. Go back to the dance. I want you guys to know that ..." I hesitate but then continue, "I've decided to accept the early admission to NYU. I'm going to finish up my high school courses. It's something I have to do and I'm not coming back. Grammy has a friend that lives in Brooklyn. I will be staying with her until I can move into the dorms. We have a month left of high school, guys, and I need a change of scenery. Don't be mad, please."

"Holy shit! I can't believe that we won't be together anymore. God, I'm going to miss you so much, but I am incredibly proud of you." Tears prick Marley's eyes. She's not the emotional one in the group, so this makes my decision even harder. Am I sure?

"I love you both so much. This is something I have to do." With those words, my confidence and certainty grows stronger. I know this is the right way to go. "We can video chat and you guys can come to NYU. It will be different, but we're soul sisters and that will never change. Go back and have fun. Come over tomorrow for breakfast. We can talk more then."

"You mean say goodbye," Cassie says, her face dotted with tears.

"No goodbyes, just see you later," I say with conviction.

"That's incredibly cheesy, Nina. You can do better than that," Marley quips.

I laugh while squeezing their hands and say, "Go have fun. Please don't broadcast my leaving. I don't want anyone to know until I'm gone."

"Okay. Your secret is in our vault. Oh, we'll have fun alright. Cassie, let's go fuck with Harrison and Melanie."

They look at each other with debauchery in their eyes. Yeah, my friends rock, and God help their targets.

We hug and I get in the car to leave feeling a little more hopeful, thanks to my friends.

Harrison

I thought that maybe I could talk to Nina and make her understand. I mean, I can try to rationalize this all day long, but the reality is she's right. I have no balls to stand up to my parents. Everything is on their terms. It's killing me that I hurt her, and it's killing me that I'm so powerless. What kind of life am I going to have if it's this hard now?

I called her. Left messages. Tried to get her friends to talk to me, but nothing. So now I'm headed to her house to take her on face-to-face. She's going to have to listen to me, and I'll … probably take a beating.

I swallow and knock on the door to her house. It opens and I'm greeted by her very unhappy-looking grandmother. If I'm completely honest, I'm surprised she doesn't have a shotgun aimed at my head.

"Hello, ma'am. I was hoping to speak to Nina. I came to apologize to her." Her gaze terrifies me, and I realize I'm shaking. I mean, I'm pretty built and I'm shaking. Maybe Nina was right with her "no balls" comment.

"Well, even if she was here, I wouldn't let you in the front door. What kind of person does what you did to her? I really don't need an answer. You're simply a coward."

"I agree with you, what I did was stupid, and I'm willing to wait until she gets home to talk to her. I need to make this right."

Her eyes become glassy as she looks at me. "She won't be home. NYU offered her early admission since she's nearly finished with her high school requirements and could graduate early. She left this morning. Thank you for helping her make that decision. Before the prom, she was waffling because of you."

With that she shuts the door in my face. The only decision I ever made for myself was asking her to prom, talking to her, getting to know her better, and now ... I'm left spiraling.

Nina

Fifteen Years Later

This man is infuriating. Sitting in first class, Harrison looks like he walked off the cover of *GQ*, sipping his bourbon and generally annoying me. Oh, he isn't doing anything to me, it's just his presence. His ability to get under my skin. "Ugh." Great. I said that out loud.

"Problem, Nina?" He smirks.

"No problem. Could you possibly turn down the volume on your drinking?"

"What? That's ridiculous. You can't turn down the volume on drinking. I don't even know what that means." His brow furrows as he looks at me.

"The clinking of your ice in the glass and your sipping is too loud. Those are just two examples."

"Is my breathing too loud?"

He's teasing me. Even I know I'm being ridiculous, but I can't admit that to him. How am I ever going to survive this trip with him? *Focus.* This isn't about me. It's about celebrating my best friend's engagement.

I mean, I kind of deserve credit since I did initially introduce them. I always knew they would be perfect together.

Harrison's voice jolts me out of my thoughts. "I asked you a question. Is my breathing too loud?"

"Well, your chattiness certainly isn't quiet," I scoff.

"I can't win with you. Look, we've got to agree on a truce. I know that you're angry with me, but I can't change what happened all those years ago. This is about our friends. Let's try to get along."

I hate it when he's reasonable. Unfortunately, he is right. I guess I can fake it until I make it there. Thank God there will be copious amounts of wine.

"Are we in agreement?" he asks.

"Yes, we're in agreement," I whisper.

"Wait, did you just agree with me, because I couldn't hear you. I guess my drinking is a lot louder than I originally thought." He laughs at his own joke.

"You heard me. I'm not repeating myself. I love Addie and Jameson, so I'll be nice. For now."

"Maybe, Nina, just maybe we can reconcile our feelings while we're there." Before I can say anything, he puts his earbuds in and deliberately shakes his ice cubes in a rhythmic fashion.

No way. Reconciling my feelings is exactly what frightens me.

Nina

Three Months Later

"Do you think it's stylish to pick a dress with pockets?" my best friend, Addie, inquires. We are literally drowning in bridal magazines as she peruses every last page, trying to plan her wedding to the love of her life. I'm proud to say I was the matchmaker.

I drift away from her question, thinking about her journey to becoming a best-selling author. Her first book was a rousing success, and I knew that she needed a publicist. I hired the brooding, hot Jameson knowing that he would be just the challenge she needed. Who am I kidding? They challenged each other, and the electrical charge in the air when they were together was undeniable. I smile every time I think of all they have been through and their commitment to each other. He even gave up his apartment in the city for her apartment in Brooklyn so her brother, Owen, who has Down syndrome, wouldn't have to give up his job at the neighborhood grocery store. That's love. His relationship with Owen is so sweet. Oh, and I am apparently Owen's girlfriend. At least, that's what he tells everyone. Honestly, he's the closest thing to having one. I don't do relationships.

"Um, are you even listening? I mean, I *am* the bride. This is really about me and you're being so selfish?" she deadpans. Addie is not a bridezilla. In fact, if it were up to her, they would simply go down to the courthouse, but Owen is totally stoked about being the best man, and Addie can't deny her brother. "You seem a tad distracted. Are you having sex and haven't shared with the class?" she quips.

"No action, my friend. I've been too busy helping someone plan her wedding." I grin at her.

"It's me, right? Because if someone else has taken my place, I will cut them." She takes her finger and slides it across her neck. I laugh.

"Of course it's you. Now, pockets in the dress? Do I need to ask? Are you thinking about a place to put your sweets, sweet?" I know my Addie. She must have a stash of chocolate available when she's nervous. Seriously, it's her version of Xanax.

"Duh. Of course. The last time I was wearing an outfit that didn't have pockets, I stashed some in my bra. Long story short, they melted and Jameson ended up licking—"

I interrupt because I really don't need to hear the rest.

"TMI, Addie. Now, let's put down these magazines and go get a drink. It's Friday night and I need to find a little release." She laughs at me.

"Okay, let's go. I'll text Jameson to meet us there. Maybe he'll bring Harrison." She wiggles her eyebrows at me. I roll my eyes. Are you wondering if she's talking about the same Harrison who annoyed me during the whole flight over to Italy for their engagement celebration? Well, it is indeed. Fuck. My. Life.

Nina

Eleven Years Ago

As I walk out of my first meeting as a literary agent, I can't help but smile. Graduating from NYU and interning at one of the biggest publishing houses in the city opened a lot of doors for me. And here I am, Nina Bryant, small-town girl making her mark in the big city. Success is the sweetest revenge.

Am I still bitter about what happened with Harrison? Yes. I know I probably should have gotten over it, but it has shaped every relationship I've ever attempted. Guys say I'm cold, detached, and aloof. My guard is up, and I have a difficult time letting people in, which is why my circle is small. Grammy says I need to open my heart, but I don't know if that's possible. So I spend my time hanging out with guys who aren't interested in a relationship. Both parties know the score, so no harm, no foul.

I open the door to the dimly lit bar where I'm meeting my former college roommate, Raquel Lancaster. When she enters a room, every eye looks at her. No lie. She is drop-dead gorgeous. Luscious red locks that flow down her back draw attention to her body, which rivals

Marilyn Monroe's. The best thing about her is that she has no idea the effect she has on people, especially men.

Making my way through the crowd of professionals unwinding from their day, I find a corner table and settle in. I order a dirty martini from the waitress who pops by, then check my email. When I look up, Raquel is approaching in her chic designer dress that enhances her assets. Trust me, she has some big assets, and they don't go unnoticed. I think every male *and* female in the bar is watching her. Then I see a man behind her clutching her hand. It isn't a surprise as, while I adore her, she seems to forget what "girls' night out" entails. Just us ladies gathering to drink and gossip. I put on a fake smile as they approach, and before Raquel can introduce her male companion, I gasp. After all these years, I'm face-to-face with Harrison. The universe must be bored. Fuck. My. Life.

His fitted suit hugs his tall, muscular frame. The good-looking boy has become a really hot man. Damn. His jet-black hair is thick and wavy, begging for my fingers to run through it. His chiseled face is accentuated by his damn dimples. And seriously, you could be blinded by the gleam of his white teeth. Why couldn't he have a beer belly, or perhaps a receding hairline?

When I came to New York, I changed my whole persona. No longer a shy, awkward young girl, I evolved with an edge. I quickly learned that my edge allows me to protect myself and navigate a male-dominated world. Only my Grammy and close friends get the warm and loving side of me. Plus, I'm prettier than I was in high school. What? It's true. I mean, I don't want to toot my own horn, but some men refer to me as "hot" and "unattainable." Which I am. The longest relationship I've had was for one month, and that was only because the sex was good. When I couldn't commit on an emotional level, we parted ways.

I see Harrison's eyes widen and his smile falter a bit. Good, he's uncomfortable. This might be fun.

"Nina, I am so sorry I'm late. I wanted you to meet Harrison. Harrison, this is my friend and former college roommate, Nina." She settles in next to Harrison while stroking his arm incessantly. Our eyes meet. Why couldn't he have been hit with an ugly bat? Jesus, he's more attractive than he was in high school.

"So, are you in transition, Harrison?" I ask. Confusion blankets his face.

"I'm sorry, what?"

"I'm not sure if I'm being politically correct, but this is *girls'* night out, so I wondered if you were in transition to becoming a female."

"God, Nina! You're so rude sometimes. I met Harrison last week at a charity dinner, and we've been having a little fun together." Her eyes twinkle with lust. I roll my eyes. Typical Raquel with her twisted sense of loyalty. I can't fault her since she doesn't know our background, but even if she did, she would prefer to side with her flavor of the week.

"Oh, well, in that case, I apologize for inferring you were in the market to get a vagina." The moment the words come out of my mouth, I regret them.

"Nina, trust me when I say that I am *always* in the market for a good vagina." He grins at me and I simply want to be invisible. I glare.

"If you'll excuse me, I need to get home. I have some work to do before I meet with a client tomorrow." I chug the rest of my martini and get up from the table.

"We just got here. Don't go, Nina," Raquel whines.

"Enjoy your evening. Raquel, I'll talk to you tomorrow. Harrison, a pleasure meeting you." I turn and move through the crowd to leave. As I get to the door, I feel a hand on my arm. I turn around to see who it is and am greeted by the piercing eyes of my archnemesis. The boy who broke my heart.

Harrison

I'm not sure why I agreed to come. I met Raquel last week at a dinner and, well, to be honest, I was horny, and she was there. We've been hooking up ever since. Women know the score with me. I don't do long-term. I don't get involved. It's too messy. Plus, I'm in the midst of growing my business as a publicist, so my time is spent networking and promoting my clients. I don't have time to be distracted with a relationship.

Raquel is rattling on about whatever—I don't really listen—as we walk toward the table to meet her friend. As we approach, I can barely contain my surprise. There, in front of me, is the only girl who ever captured my heart: Nina Bryant.

After she left, I was lost. I know we were never together, but she did something no one else has ever done. She got under my skin. And now, as I look at her, I'm overwhelmed by her beauty. She's stunning. Nina was always pretty, both inside and out, but this grown-up version takes my breath away. I start to smile at her, but her icy demeanor stops me.

"Nina, I am so sorry I'm late. I wanted you to meet Harrison. Harrison, this is my friend and former college roommate, Nina." Our eyes meet. She is breathtaking.

"So, are you in transition, Harrison?" she asks. I don't know what she's talking about.

"I'm sorry, what?" Nina is acting as if she doesn't remember me, or maybe this is her game. Okay, I'll play.

"I'm not sure if I'm being politically correct, but this is *girls'* night out, so I wondered if you were in transition to becoming a female." She is snarky, sassy, and I am so captivated by her. The shame of how I treated her blankets me. Where is that shy girl? Did I break her?

"God, Nina! You are so rude sometimes. I met Harrison last week at a charity dinner, and we've been having a little fun together." She looks at me with lust, but it's hard to return that look when the girl I always wanted is sitting right across from me. Raquel grabs my hand on the table. Nina rolls her eyes. Raquel is fun, but this isn't going to go the distance, and I think she might be catching feelings. I shudder with the thoughtand release her hand. She scowls at me, but all I do is shrug.

"Oh, well, in that case, I apologize for inferring you were in the market to get a vagina." Nina's face reddens.

"Nina, trust me when I say that I am *always* in the market for a good vagina." I grin at her and give her my signature wink. She glares at me.

"If you'll excuse me, I need to get home. I have some work to do before I meet with a client tomorrow." She throws back the rest of her martini and gets up from the table. I can't let her leave. The intense need to be a part of her life is palpable. The only obstacle is her.

"We just got here. Don't go, Nina," Raquel pleads. Her whine is annoying.

"Enjoy your evening. Raquel, I'll talk to you tomorrow. Harrison, a pleasure meeting you." She turns and starts toward the door. I excuse myself and follow her. Raquel looks confused, but I can't worry about that now. There is this pull I have toward Nina, and I need to find out why she's acting this way. Prom was a long time ago. Could she still be mad?

I put my hand on her arm as she inches her way through the crowd. "Nina, wait."

She turns toward me, her eyes cold and detached. I search for any inkling of the sweet, shy girl I used to know.

"Can I help you?"

"How's your grammy?" I blurt, knowing that the mention of her beloved grandmother will calm her. Her face softens a little and her eyes sparkle.

"She's good. Thank you for asking. Now if you don't mind, I'm leaving."

"Nina, I don't know what that little act was all about, but I would like to catch up. Do you want to do dinner some time?" My internal dialogue is chanting, "Say yes!" I just need a sign, any sign at all. Her face has turned to stone again, her beautiful features emotionless.

"No, thank you. Take care of yourself." And with that she walks out of my life once again.

Nina

Have you ever planned a verbal attack on a person who has wronged you? Don't lie. I think it's perfectly natural to want to express sharp words. To stand up for yourself. For the last eleven years, I knew exactly what I would say to Harrison if we ever met again. Guess what happened? I choked. Blindsided by his beauty and his easy smile, I was transfixed. Plus, he was with one of my friends in a "romantic" fashion, so that put a damper on my plan.

As I get into my cab, I look back to see him staring at me. I won't deny my attraction or the spark I felt being in his presence. But I can't allow myself to feel that pull. Shit, I thought I could escape the rush of emotions that bubbled up being in his presence. That I had secured myself enough not to feel. Feeling hurts. Feeling powerless. It's the act of free-falling, something I won't allow myself to do.

I know what you're going to say. You want to tell me it isn't healthy not to feel. That I need to let go of the past. You're probably right. Maybe one day I'll get there, but not now. I'm still reeling from seeing him again.

Nina

Present Day–Four Years Later

A ddie and I arrive at the bar and await two of the most gorgeous men I have ever seen. I really hate to admit I like to look at Harrison. His chiseled face, muscular build, firm ass, and his lips that beg to be kissed. Woah. Is it hot in here?

It's a lot of work to be around him. He challenges me. He annoys me. But there is no way to escape him. He owns the biggest public relations agency in New York, and my clients deserve the best. Then, on top of it all, the universe—who, by the way, is a bitter bitch that enjoys finding humor in my discomfort—brings him into my circle of friends. He is best friends with Jameson, who's set to marry my best friend, Addie. Sigh.

We settle into a booth, which forces me to sit next to him. Our thighs are touching. His woodsy scent tickles my noise, and don't get me started on those ridiculous chocolate eyes. If only I could release the feelings I still have for him. I won't allow myself to be vulnerable. Ever. Been there, done that. That girl is gone. Addie startles me back into reality.

"Isn't this fun? I am so happy you guys could hang out with us tonight." Addie's grin widens. She is so ridiculously happy that it sometimes borders on annoying. Okay, I sound like an ass, but I would never tell her that. No crime in having those thoughts.

"Absolutely! So much fun." I grit my teeth anxiously, looking for the waitress. A cocktail needs to appear pronto. Thank God she gets to our table quickly and shimmies up to the table, eyeing Harrison.

"What can I get you?" Her voice is breathy. I roll my eyes.

"I would love a bourbon, neat. Top shelf, please. You pick, doll." He winks at her. She blushes. I clear my throat to get her attention, and she glares at me.

"And for you?" I'm an afterthought apparently. So much for "ladies first."

"I would adore a dry martini made with Tanqueray Gin served in a chilled glass with two olives." I smile my fake smile, reserved only for assholes. She turns, not really acknowledging my order, asking Jameson and Addie what they would like to drink. What the hell? Oh, wait. I get it. She thinks I'm with Harrison. As if. Whatever. She'll probably spit in my drink or, God forbid, have it made with some cheap gin.

Harrison is staring at me.

"What?" I snap.

"Nothing. I just didn't take you for a martini girl." He shrugs.

"Just because I didn't grow up with a silver spoon stuck up my ass, you think I can't enjoy a sophisticated drink," I bite back.

"First, the spoon was in my mouth, and second, every time I have been out with you, you seem to order an expensive glass of wine. I was just surprised at the change."

"Well, Harrison, you don't know me. Besides, some occasions call for the strong stuff."

Fortunately, our drinks arrive in no time. She puts down Harrison's first, then Addie's, then Jameson's. When she finally serves mine, the liquid sloshes from side to side. It isn't what I ordered either. Before I can react to the frothy, fruity, disgusting concoction in front of me, Harrison says, "Doll, she ordered a dry martini with Tanqueray Gin, two olives, in a chilled glass." He hands her my drink. "Can you correct that for me, please?" He smiles at her. It's his sexy smile. The fact that I know that pisses me off.

She is flustered. Her cheeks become pink. "Well, of course I can do that." She doesn't look at me or even apologize. I'm growing angrier that he felt the need to step in. Before I can even say anything, Addie grabs my hand. She knows that I'm about to blow. She nods and I raise my eyebrow. Silent communication is our thing. I surrender. She's good at grounding me.

"Okay, we have something to ask you guys." She beams at us. "We want you guys to be in our wedding. Nina, will you be my maid of honor? I can't imagine my wedding without you by my side."

My anger toward Harrison dissipates, and I squeeze her hand. "Of course. I would be honored to stand with you." Tears cloud my eyes.

"What about me? Are there going to be any hot bridesmaids?" And just like that, my anger meter goes through the roof. Typical. Always taking a sweet moment and making it dirty. Bastard.

"Well, if you had any amount of patience, I was going to ask you to be my co-best man? With that comes the responsibility of being Owen's wingman." Jameson laughs.

"I would be happy to be your co-best man and equally thrilled to help Owen with the ladies." He wiggles his eyebrows.

"Awesome! It's all settled. So, we're getting married in two months on a beach in Antigua. Oh, and the joint bachelor/bachelorette party will be in Vegas four weeks before the big day!" Addie is using jazz hands and I'm in need of alcohol. At that moment, my cocktail arrives, thank goodness. Perfectly prepared, of course, because *he* ordered it. I chug it and smile at Addie.

"Can't wait!"

Not one but two trips paired with Harrison sounds like a recipe for disaster. And don't get me started on Vegas. The last time I was there, I made the biggest mistake of my life.

Harrison

I watch Nina's fist clench as she delivers her fake smile. The one that doesn't reach her eyes. She is incredibly beautiful when she's flustered. Annoyed. My favorite pastime is getting a rise out of her. It's the only time when I feel like she's transparent. Vulnerable. I had some news to share with her, but I figure the realization that we'll be paired in a wedding in a remote location is enough for one evening. Or is it?

Now, I know you're probably wondering what the news is. Would it be fair to share that information before she reads it in her mail when she gets home? I bet her screams will reverberate throughout the city. I grin at the thought.

"What are you grinning about?" I'm jolted out of my devious thoughts by Jameson's impatient voice. Nina is looking at me like I'm crazy. She and Addie excuse themselves to go to the restroom. I guess I was grinning like a lunatic. Whatever.

"Nothing. Just thinking about your wedding. Happy for you, man."

"Thanks. Now that I'm off the market, let's talk about you. You know, the chemistry between you and Nina is combustible. When are you going to admit there's something there?"

"Just because you've been touched by the love fairy, it doesn't mean you have to drag me into your bliss. I'm happy for you, but I'm good." It kind of sounds like I'm trying to convince myself. Jameson cocks his head like he doesn't believe me. Hell, I don't know if I believe it myself.

"You're my best friend, and yet you've never told me how you know Nina. It's obvious you have a history. Care to share with the class?" *That*, my friends, is an Addie expression. She has really rubbed off on Jameson. And his smug expression is annoying me. No, I haven't shared our history. Despite the whole thing happening years ago, I'm still ashamed of how I acted, but I'm not about to admit that out loud. That it still haunts me to this day. That I wish I could change the past.

"That's a story for another time." I chug the rest of my drink and get up to leave.

Nina and Addie return to the table. "Leaving so soon?" Nina asks, looking a little too pleased.

"Yep, I have an early morning. By the way, you should be receiving something in your mail that I know you're going to love." I smirk. She frowns.

I hug a confused Addie and shake Jameson's hand. I walk out the door feeling lighter than I have in years.

Nina

"What the hell does he mean?" Addie inquires. I shrug. "Who knows with him? His favorite hobby is to annoy me." My mind is swirling over what he said, and now I'm desperately curious to know what's waiting in my mail. I grab my stuff. "Early morning, friends. So happy for you, but I need to get home."

Addie laughs. "Someday you're going to tell me the story of how you two know each other. We *know* there is a history." I love my friend, but there's no way in hell I'm going to share the humiliation that was my high school prom experience with her. I just want to forget about that part of my life. I don't even want anyone to see me as I was; I'm who I am now, that's all.

"No story there at all."

"Ha! You're a terrible liar. That means the story is really good. You won't be able to avoid telling me forever. I am relentless. Maybe I'll sic Owen on you." She grins.

"You know I can't resist Owen." God, I love that young man so much. I hug Addie and Jameson, then walk out the door.

I flag a cab and it delivers me to my two-bedroom apartment in the West Village. Opening the door to my home, I breathe a sigh of relief. Once I made my mark as a literary agent, I invested wisely and bought this cozy space. This is my sanctuary where I can just be Nina, not the hard-nosed, cold professional I show the world.

I drop my keys on the counter and go through the mail like a crazy lady. I can't imagine what could be so riveting that Harrison would intentionally vaguespeak. It's a thing. Trust me. Like vagueposting on social media. Vaguespeaking exists. Harrison is the king of it. Why does he continue to get under my skin? The real question is why I continue to allow it.

I sort through and, like a snake hiding in the bushes ready to attack, I see it: an invitation. Not just any invitation. It's an invitation to our fifteen-year high school reunion. He knew how this would make me feel. Part of me wants to go so I can show those smug assholes how successful I am. The other part wants to resort to eating a copious amount of ice cream and hunkering down in my apartment. I have dueling personalities. Sigh.

My cell rings and I see it's Grammy calling. Of course she's calling. She'll give me a pep talk and then guilt me into coming because, aside from my quick pop-ins to see her, I haven't spent a lot of time in the small-minded town of crushed dreams. Population under 5,000. Might have gotten bigger, but I try not to keep up. Grammy enjoys gossiping about various people, but honestly, I barely listen. Harrison and I seem to be the only ones who left that hellhole. Wish he had gone somewhere else.

"Hi, Grammy!" I try to put a smile in my voice.

"You got the invitation, didn't you?" I can never hide anything from her.

"Yes, I did, but I'm not going." I sound like a petulant child.

"Girl, when are you going to let this high school thing go? It didn't define you. It shaped you into this amazing woman. Plus, don't you want to rub it in their faces?" She giggles.

I laugh because while Grammy is the kindest soul on the plant, she is a loyal badass. "I thought you loved everyone in the name of Jesus?" I tease.

"Not when they're assholes. Come home. Come stay with me. Take a week off. I know you can. I talked to Lillie and she can make it happen. Please. I'm not getting any younger and I just want to see my beautiful granddaughter." Damn. My assistant Lillie is a traitorous bitch. Add in Grammy with her whole guilt trip, you have the dream team for manipulation.

I weigh my options, but all in all, Grammy is right. "Okay, I'll come, but it isn't because of you going behind my back to Lillie or because of the guilt trip. This is my decision."

"Of course it is, sweetie. Let me know your travel plans. I'll cook all your favorites. Honey, this will be good for you. It's called closure, and you desperately need it."

We say goodbye, and I'm left alone with my thoughts. Maybe she's right. At some point, I need to move on and let this shit go. I think the universe has a twisted sense of humor because as it stands now, I will be thrown together with Harrison more times than I care to be. How am I supposed to move on if I'm stuck with him, or is that the point?

Nina

I pop into the Starbucks near my office the next morning. A caffeine fix is necessary. The sun is shining, and I do have a little pep in my step despite the doom of my high school reunion hanging over me like a dark cloud. While I wait for my order, my phone buzzes and it's Addie. I laugh to myself because I know exactly what she wants.

"Good morning, Addie."

"Well, what was it? What was in the mail? Did it make you mad? Have you talked to Harrison?"

"Jesus, Addie, take a breath."

"Sorry. I'm dying here. Literally dying to find out what mystery mail you got."

"Well, Nancy Drew, it wasn't a big deal."

Silence.

"Are you going to tell me or not?" Her tone is laced with annoyance.

"Let's meet for lunch. We need to go over your tour for your new book anyway."

Addie wrote a memoir that is going to blow its way through the bestseller list: her story of persistence and strength after finding out her father, who abandoned her in the first place, wasn't her father after all. Her real father is a senator, and trust me, it was a crazy turn of events that brought all this about, including her cousin-in-law Dorothy orchestrating the whole circus.

"You're just going to use lunch as a distraction." She uses her pouty voice.

I roll my eyes and sigh. "I promise I'll tell you what was in the mail, okay?"

"Oh goody! I can't wait. Does Harrison need to come for the publicity stuff?"

Now that she and Jameson are engaged, Harrison took over the duty of being her publicist. They want to keep work separate from their relationship.

"Nope. I'll email him the particulars."

"Can we go to that bistro near your office? They have the best truffle fries."

My best friend loves her food. I'm more cautious with what I eat. I shudder at the processed foods she ingests.

"Of course we can. I think there's something I can eat there."

She cackles. This girl.

"Oh yes, my little health nut, there's that kale salad you always order."

"I forgot about that. Does noon work? I'll have Lillie make reservations."

"Noon is perfect. Speaking of Lillie, I gave her the dates for Vegas and Antigua, so you're all set. See you then. Be prepared to spill your guts."

Is Lillie *my* assistant or is she available for the general population?

"See you then!"

As I hang up, I realize that I'm going to have to tell Addie the whole story of my history with Harrison. Maybe this will be therapeutic. Maybe I should have suggested drinks instead.

Nina

I enter the building where my office is located and smile. I love my job and I love this city. At least one area of my life is going well. I shake my head at the thought. Grammy is probably right about me letting go of the past. Maybe I could if the past weren't shoved in my face all the time. I am so lost in thought that I have no recollection of getting on the elevator and arriving on my floor. I really need to get my head in the game.

I step off the elevator and greet our receptionist, Amy. Right now, I employ ten literary agents along with five assistants. We're growing steadily, and I am so proud of our accomplishments. I stop at Lillie's desk before entering my office.

"Any fires I need to put out this morning?" I ask.

Lillie is engrossed in something I hope is work related.

"Lillie?" I arch my eyebrow at her.

She looks up at me sheepishly and minimizes her distraction. "I'm sorry. I didn't hear you."

Lillie has been with me from the very beginning. I met her while she was a waitress at a bar near NYU. She reminds me of a tiny fairy with her petite frame and pert nose. Her warm smile and easygoing attitude soften my edginess and abrasiveness. She is the yin to my yang. Anyway, I would go to that bar after my internship with a bunch of people from the agency. One night, we started having a conversation about life and goals. She shared that she was a single mom to a little girl with autism and needed to find a job that had daytime hours with benefits. The more we talked, the more I realized that her talents were being wasted and that she would be perfect as my assistant. Granted, I wasn't even a literary agent yet, but I knew my path forward, and she would be part of it.

"What has you so distracted? Is it our new client, Benjamin Morris? He's kind of a tool, so if he's harassing you, let me know."

"Um, no, it isn't anything like that." She isn't making eye contact with me, which is so unlike her.

"Lillie, tell me. I promise I won't be mad. Are you looking for another job? I swear to God I will cut the person who wants to hire you. Please don't leave me. I'm ready to beg."

"Jesus, Nina. I'm not leaving you, but good to know that you're so desperate to keep me. No, I was returning a message on a dating site. There. I said it. I'm trying to date. I apologize for using company time for my personal business." Her cheeks sprinkle with pink and her eyes glisten with unshed tears. She's scared.

"Lillie, sweetie, I'm not mad at you. Surprised since I haven't heard you discuss dating, though. Why the sudden shift?" Maybe her insight can help me with my own situation.

"Well, I just need to have something that doesn't involve being a mother or being an employee. I want to feel like a woman again. Do you know how long it's been since I was touched by a man? Not sex per se, but holding hands or even a hug? Eons! I can't even remember. My friend Candance told me about a new dating site that takes the pressure off with rules that say you can't meet until you have exchanged messages for four weeks."

"What? That sounds weird."

"It's called Get 2 Know Me, and it encourages dialogue between interested parties before the initial meeting. You complete a profile, and then the program matches you based on your interests. Then you can start exchanging messages through the site. There are no photos allowed in your messages, so you can really get to know someone. Then after four weeks, you can decide to meet or not."

"So you don't get dick pics or any other sordid type of obscene photos?"

She nods.

"And after four weeks, if you like someone, you meet them?" I can't believe I'm entertaining this.

"Yes. The theory is that after you've gotten to know someone for that long, you know each other on a deeper level. It's supposed to take the awkwardness out of the first personal meeting."

"Oh."

"That's it? All you can say is *oh*? I know it sounds unconventional, but I really am optimistic about it. I'm three weeks in, and I've connected with this guy called Gabe. He's a single parent, too, so he gets the frustration of being alone in the parenting process."

"What if the person is lying? I'm not saying this Gabe guy is, but what if they aren't being truthful, and you've wasted four weeks getting to know them?"

"Nina, what if they aren't and they're your ideal match? It's called taking a leap of faith, and I'll be honest with you. If I don't take some chances, I will live with regret. I don't want that added to my already heavy baggage."

"Fair enough. Just be careful."

"I will. And Nina? I'm happy to help you set up a profile." She winks at me.

"That won't be necessary. I'm happy with the way things are," I lie. "Oh, and thanks so much for meddling in my life and committing me to going home to that horrid high school reunion."

"You're welcome! And it really is about seeing your grammy, not the reunion."

"Ugh, you and your guilt trip. Well, I can see the two of you will get along just fine. In fact, why don't you and Maddie come for a bit? It might be good to get away, and I know Grammy would love to meet you both. Especially since you're now her coconspirator."

"Really? I think that would be fun! Okay, we'll come. Thank you for inviting us." She grins.

"You're welcome. It's penance for conspiring against me. Can you make the arrangements? I am going to Grammy's first, then Vegas, back to West Virginia, and then to Antigua from there."

"Well, at least you have Vegas and Antigua to look forward to, and spending a few days with your grandmother before you go to Sin City will be a good thing. See? You always need to look on the bright side of life."

"Lillie, did you seriously just quote Monty Python?"

She grins at me. "I did indeed. Nina, just so you know, I sent the link for the dating app to your email. You can thank me later." She laughs and I scowl.

Why does everyone think they know what's best for me?

Nina

I settle into my routine of responding to emails, touching base with clients, and the usual, but there is this magnetic feeling that I can't seem to shake. Maybe a dating app couldn't hurt. Maybe I'm done with the hump and dump portion of my life. I know that sounds crass, but it has been my pattern for years. I own it. My mouse hovers over the link. I close my eyes and click. I can do this.

As I read the fine print, I'm enthralled by the concept. No names. No pictures. Just a nickname and true conversation. It's like the online version of *The Voice* but without Blake Shelton fighting over people. Although I wouldn't mind him fighting over me ...

Focus, Nina.

The idea is to get to know someone before seeing what they look like. The whole concept is a bit unconventional, but I give them an A for effort. I set up my profile. Why am I doing this at work with no liquid courage? Oh well, I suppose it's better to do it with sound mind. The thought of this high school reunion has really cost me my sanity.

Am I truly ready to have a relationship? Is it time for me to move forward? I have no idea, but I guess this is one way for me to find out.

Harrison

My thoughts are gnawing at me. Why would I think she would call once she saw what was waiting for her in the mail? I'm an asshole. I know it. I just want her to let this petty angst between us go. Maybe if she attends, then she'll see that people change. Maybe I could get a glimpse of the carefree, kindhearted girl she once was—if that girl still exists. My lips curve remembering what she was like back then.

The lunchroom is crowded, and even though I hear my name being called over and over, I'm only looking for one person. Ever since I asked her to prom, I want to hang out with her. Get to know her. There's something alluring about her. Alluring? I sound like an old man. Anyway, there is this draw to her.

I see her. She's sitting with her cousin. Not surprising. She's fiercely protective of Mason. Some kids say he's "retarded," which I hate, but I also heard that he's autistic. And because some kids are cruel, he happens to be the target of bullying, which sometimes makes her a target by default.

I walk over to their table and put my tray down. Her face is blanketed in confusion. I smile at her and she softens.

"Why are you sitting here?"

"Hello to you too! I just thought since we're going to prom, we should get to know each other. Maybe go out on a date."

"You want to date me?"

"Sure." I shrug and take a bite out of my burger.

Her eyes linger on me. "You want to date … me. Why?"

This girl has no idea how amazing she is. Mason is eyeing me.

"I think you're cool and I think we would have fun. It's pretty simple. Mason, do you think your cousin should give me a chance?" I haven't actually spoken to him before, but I'm hoping I can get him on my side.

"Dating involves sexual tension and emotions. Teenagers are statistically known to be impulsive and forge ahead with a sexual relationship before they are emotionally capable of handling the consequences." He breaks eye contact and resumes eating. I am rendered speechless. Okay. Guess that's a no to teen dating.

I look back at Nina.

"I'll think about it." She gives me a soft smile.

"I'll take that answer for now.

I spend the rest of the day with a grin on my face.

"Why the grin?" Jameson inquires. I wonder how long he's been standing there.

"Can't a guy smile without the inquisition?"

"Not you. You usually aren't a smiley kind of guy." He laughs.

"Just happy to be alive. I'm coordinating Addie's book-tour schedule. Just waiting on Nina." I desperately want the subject to change.

"You do know that I actually live with the woman and that we share everything. For example, she told me that Nina was going to spill the story behind the two of you."

Well, fuckety fuck.

"Is she now?"

"You seem … well, a bit nervous. Why is that?"

"I'm not nervous, you're nervous," I sputter.

"That doesn't even make sense. Look, I'm here if you want to talk. No judgement. I owe you, man." His face grows serious. Jameson went through a dark time after he served as a Navy SEAL and was injured while on a mission. His mom passed away while he was gone, and all of that mess peppered with a case of PTSD sent him into a dark depression. I stayed with him through it all. He is my brother. He's more my family than the one that raised me.

"I hear you, man. I appreciate it. Not much to tell, but when I'm ready, I'll share it with you." And I really mean it.

"Alright, talk to you later. I'm meeting with that new client, Portia Robinson. She's a social media influencer, which I think is bullshit, but whatever pays her bills and mine." He laughs and walks out the door, leaving me with my memories of Nina.

Nina

I don't usually dread a lunch, but boy am I not looking forward to sharing my past with Addie. I just hate reliving it. I'm ashamed that I was vulnerable. I'm ashamed that I allowed someone to reside in my heart. Most of all, I hate that I have feelings for him even after what happened.

I walk into the cozy bistro, where I find Addie at a corner table. The restaurant is quiet, but most of all, private. She already has a plate of truffle fries in front of her, and I'm not even late. I grin at her. She's probably the one person who easily removes my armor.

"Couldn't wait for me?" I laugh as she gets up to hug me with a fry hanging out of her mouth.

"You know this is my weakness, but don't worry, this is just my appetizer. Do you need a cocktail before we dive right into your juicy story, or are you good with water?" She smirks.

She knows that I cringe at the thought of tap water. Sparkling with a lemon and lime is my drink of choice when I'm not indulging in a cocktail.

"Kidding, of course. I ordered you both. Your dirty martini in a chilled glass with top- shelf gin and two olives, along with sparkling water served with lemon and lime are on their way. Not judging, but you are kind of a drink snob." She chuckles.

"You know when you say 'not judging,' you are, in fact, judging. I don't consider myself a snob. I simply know what I like, so thank you for ordering both. I do have to go back to work after we're done, so I'll just stick with the nonalcoholic choice."

Addie waves me off. "I talked to Lillie and she rescheduled your afternoon. I told her our lunch would take a while. I didn't want you to feel rushed."

My eyes bug out at her. "What is the deal with everyone in my life calling Lillie to make decisions that I should be making myself? I had important appointments this afternoon." My voice is laced with irritation.

"Calm your tits, Nina. I think your lady bits are pissed that you haven't had any action, and whatever is going on with Harrison has your panties all twisty."

"First of all, my tits are calm, and let's not discuss my vagina. Seriously, I haven't even had a drink of my martini yet." I look around for the waitress, wishing my drink would magically appear. As if she read my mind, the deliciousness is set in front of me. I take a gulp and sigh with relief. So much for not drinking during day.

"Okay, spill." She leans forward, eager to hear my tale of woe.

"This is between us, right? No sharing with Jameson."

She looks at me as if I slapped her. "Nina, of course I won't tell him. But remember, he was a Navy SEAL. He has ways of making me talk, if you know what I mean." She wiggles her eyebrows at me.

"Oh, for the love of Jesus, please stop. I don't need to think of you having sex, especially when I'm having a dry spell." Crap. This martini is like a truth serum.

"Go on, Dr. Addie is in, and I'm all ears." She settles in with her fries, looking at me as if I were a movie about to start.

So, I spill. I tell her of the prom invitation. I share with her about how he wanted to date me. Somewhere between this and telling her about prom night, she orders me another drink and shoves a second round of truffle fries toward me. Sharing this stuff is hard; I make an exception to my rules and indulge in both.

Her facial expression morphs from relaxed to pissed as she grabs my hand.

"I want to cut off his balls and make him suffer," she says matter-of-factly.

I choke on my drink and giggle. "I don't think that's necessary. It was fifteen years ago, and I'm totally over it." I lie, as I am obviously not over it at all. I have just shoved it down deep along with my parents' deaths. Although I guess it can't be hidden away *that* deep if it's still affecting my life.

"Honey, you're precious, thinking that you're over it. Now, I love Harrison, but you are my sister, so what do you need me to do? I can be evil, you know."

She totally can't be evil. Addie is a big softy unless something is threatening Owen, then all bets are off.

"Actually, I might have to deal with it sooner rather than later. The mail that Harrison mentioned was an invitation to our fifteen-year high school reunion. Grammy cleared my schedule with Lillie and guilted me into going. Something about getting closure."

"I need to meet your grammy. This is going to be awesome. You get to go back and show everyone how successful and amazing you are. What are you going to wear?"

I laugh at her question about my clothes selection because early on, when her first book was published, her stylist, George, and I nearly had a nervous breakdown trying to get her to wear something other than yoga pants and T-shirts.

"I haven't thought that far ahead. But Lillie is going too. I thought it would be good for her to have a bit of a vacation. She's bringing her daughter along for the fun. I figured some Grammy time would be good for them. Oh, and the reunion is happening after Vegas."

At the mention of Lillie's daughter, Addie's face lights up. She understands the plight of raising a child with special needs. After all, she basically raised her brother, Owen, after her mother emotionally abandoned her, along with her "fake" father, who left not long after Owen was diagnosed with Down syndrome. She speaks to Lillie often—any time she calls me at the office—and has told me a few times she'd love to have Owen meet Maddie.

"Is Harrison going?" Addie inquires.

"I have no idea, but my guess is yes. His parents still live there, so I imagine it would be a good excuse to visit." I try to sound nonchalant, but I know Addie can read my face.

"Get a wax before you go. That area is probably overgrown."

"Jesus, Addie, stop talking about my vagina. And yes, I will be going to the spa, but to attend to other things," I lie, and she laughs. She knows me too well.

"Spill it." Her eyes bore into mine. I look away because I can't hide anything from her.

"Spill what?" My eyes wander to the bottom of my martini glass.

"There's something else you aren't telling me."

"I might have signed up for a dating app," I whisper.

"WHAT!" she bellows. Every head turns our way. I'm probably five shades of red, and Addie stares at me as if I'm some alien.

"Jesus, Addie. Could you be a little more discreet?"

"Sorry, I just never thought you would ever sign up for one of those sites."

"Lillie told me about it, and I thought maybe it was time to get myself out there. This one sounds better than the other ones."

I explain the concept to her. She nods as I finish, and then I reluctantly ask, "So what do you think?"

"Well, let me start by saying that I am so very proud of you for putting yourself out there. I like the concept. As a woman who doesn't fit the mold of what society deems attractive, this would be an excellent platform. It helps build a foundation first, which is really important. I just hope these guys are honest."

"Look, if Lillie is willing to risk it, then so am I. It's time I move forward. I have been so stuck in the emotional residue from high school that I feel stunted. I'm almost thirty-three and haven't ever been in a serious relationship. I think it's time."

"Well, I'm proud of you and will be happy to read all of your interactions with your potential suitors."

"That won't be necessary. I think I can handle that myself. Okay, now we've got to shift to work mode. Let's go over your schedule."

"Ugh … Work Nina is boring. At least you ate your weight in fries." She chuckles.

Nina

I go straight home after my long lunch with Addie. My delightful buzz is just enough for me to decide a nap is in order. Since Addie and Lillie sabotaged my schedule, I'm free to chill. Whatever that is. It's as though I have no control over my life anymore.

I walk into my sanctuary, aka my apartment, and my phone buzzes. A smile appears on my face as I see it's my cousin, Mason. Since we're the same age, it's easy for us to be friends. Truth be told, he saved me. He humbled me. Some would say I was his protector, but sometimes I think the roles were reversed. His muscular build, wavy black hair, and extremely good looks didn't lessen the target on his back in high school as he is on the Autism spectrum. Some kids are assholes. I should have been more of a target than he was. I was the bookworm, the nerdy girl with a skinny frame.

Our mothers are sisters. I spent a lot of time at their home growing up, and Mason's mother was just another strong, female role model who taught me to see my value. Aunt Tabby is fun, vivacious, and was the catalyst for advocating for Mason's needs. It was even more complicated in a small town with limited resources, but she managed to quiet the odds.

Now Mason is a successful computer analyst. He works from home, which is ideal with his anxiety in social situations. He has made a life for himself. And while he isn't a warm, fuzzy individual, his constant checking up on me is his way of showing his enormous capacity for love.

"Hey, cuz! What's up? I suppose you spoke to Grammy?"

"Yes, Nina. I did talk to her and she told me that you're coming to the reunion. Mom is excited to have you for a visit, too."

He didn't mention if he was going. That's probably way out of his comfort zone, but maybe, since I'm stepping into the fire, I can persuade him to be my date. It wouldn't be the first time we relied on each other to quell the loneliness of not having a lot of friends. Cassie and Marley completed our group back in high school. We've all known each other since grade school, and our loyalty to each other has never wavered, even when Marley started dating Harrison's best friend, Ben. We stuck up for each other and we stuck with each other. Even though I moved away, Marley and Cassie are still like my sisters.

"So, are you going with me? I can't do this alone." I use my sweet begging voice.

"I think you know the answer."

"Mason, come on. You won't be alone, and people change. I haven't talked to Marley and Cassie yet, but I bet they're going too. We can all go together. Just like old times." I try to add enthusiasm to my voice, but it falls flat.

"Of course they're going. It's the biggest social affair of the year. The only people they care about seeing are you and Harrison. You two are literally the only people who left town. They see *me* all the time. Well, they don't unless I go to the store, but you get my meaning."

Mason chooses to be alone. This good-looking, successful man isolates with his computer.

"Please go with me! I can't do it without you."

"Is Harrison going?" he inquires. When Mason talks, there is no inflection of emotion, so I can't tell if he's teasing me or not.

"I have no idea. Probably. Just to annoy me." I scoff.

"You do realize that not everything is about you. He does have family here and he was the most popular guy in our class. Why wouldn't he come?"

"Gee, when you say it like that, it sounds like he's some kind of celebrity." I roll my eyes for effect even though he can't see me.

"All I'm saying is that even though I stayed here, it doesn't mean I want to revisit my high school years."

"Will you think about it? I can bring you some of the scones you love from the bakery near my apartment."

Silence.

"Mason, are you still there?"

"I'm here. Bring the scones and I'll consider going."

I pump my fist in the air because if he's considering it, I've already got him halfway there. I can easily persuade him in person.

"Sounds good! I'll see you in a couple of weeks."

"That doesn't mean I'm going, you know."

"Sorry ... bad signal ... talk to you soon!"

I disconnect our call and can't help but laugh. Mason is probably scowling. My phone buzzes again with a text. As though she heard her name mentioned—it's from Cassie.

"Heard from a little birdie that someone is coming home and not hiding out at her grammy's the whole time. Get ready for an epic time, bitch! High school reunion, here we come." 🤍 🍷

I text her back with a grin.

"Yes, the little birdie, aka Grammy with a big mouth, is correct. Coming home to attend this hideous gathering where I will need copious amounts of alcohol."

"Marley and I have your back. We miss you and can't wait to see your skinny ass. You have avoided us for too long. Payback is a bitch." 😬

She is right. I have evaded everyone there, including my two best friends. The reminders are too painful.

I remember what Grammy said about me needing closure. I need to let go of the past. Maybe this visit will be therapeutic.

Nina

After talking with Mason and Cassie, I have a renewed burst of energy, so I decide to take the plunge by logging into my Get 2 Know Me account on my laptop. The goal is to not provide an overabundance of information aside from your interests. This allows you to be matched with individuals who are like-minded. It is suggested that you keep things light in the beginning, but if there's a connection, then talking about deeper things helps formulate a bond. There is no timetable set on when you should meet in person, but they suggest you give it some time—even more than the minimum of four weeks, if that feels right—in order to get to know one another. What a concept.

I already have two matches, and I can't help but feel a little giddy. My mouse hovers over the first name, which is Goliath. That's an interesting choice. Is he a selfish prick? Does he step all over the little guy in a ruthless fashion? Jesus. I have already judged him, so maybe I should move on to the second one. Interesting. The second screen name is Captain Morgan. That's adorable. It's clever and clearly not egotistical. I take a breath and start my message to him.

Me: *Hi! My name is Olive. Well, not really, because that would defeat the whole point, but anyway that's the screen name I chose.*

I hit send and grimace. My career is spent negotiating with big publishers and writing is my jam, so why was that intro text so lame? Ladies and gentlemen, I give up. With crickets playing in the background, I decide to simply close the app and move on with the rest of the day. Maybe nap or maybe drink. The possibilities are endless. Then I hear a ping. I scramble for my phone and grin like an idiot at the message.

Captain Morgan: Nice to meet you, Olive. I think that's a great choice for a screen name. I couldn't think of anything original, so I just stole the name of some rum. It seemed like a lot of pressure to think of something creative that would attract someone. I'm rambling, and that was not my intent. Sorry.

Me: *Don't apologize. I like your screen name. In fact, I picked it over another guy who selected Goliath as his. Wasn't sure what that was about, but I went and prejudged him realizing that we would have no future if I'm already critical of a screen name. LOL.*

Captain Morgan: Well, then I'm honored that I defeated Goliath. Does that make me David? Anyway, I'm looking forward to getting to know you. Do you want to set up regular times to chat? Not sure what your schedule is, but I usually finish my day up around 9 at night.

Me: *That works perfectly for me. So tomorrow at 9?*

Captain Morgan: Tomorrow at 9. Looking forward to it, Olive.

Me: *Me too, Captain Morgan.*

I close the chat window and a slight smile tugs my lips. That wasn't as bad as I thought it would be. He seems nice and funny. His nervousness made me a little more comfortable. Maybe Lillie was right about this approach. Of course, I won't admit anything to her just yet.

Harrison

The intel, from a very reliable source—okay, fine, it's Addie—tells me that Nina is going to our reunion. Addie was a tough nut to crack, but when I presented her with a warm chocolate croissant, she sang like a canary. That's a win for me.

Maybe Nina and I can reconcile the past. Move forward.

Am I excited about going home? No. Not only will I be forced to interact with people I have nothing in common with anymore, but I'll have to deal with my parents. Listen to this, their names are Bitsy and Lyle McCall. No joke. Pretentious. I opt out for holiday visits, so I don't have to have the constant reminder that I am a disappointment. Independently building a successful business clearly doesn't measure up to the expectations of my parental units.

What Nina doesn't realize is that my strained relationship with my parents has a lot do to with the night of senior prom. It was like an awakening for me. It defined my future. I realized I didn't want to live under my parents' thumb. Everything had strings. When I started my own agency, I was disinherited by my parents. Dear old Dad thought that would be an incentive to do his bidding, but he greatly underestimated me.

"This is it, Harrison. If you don't come back and fulfill your legacy, you will no longer be considered part of the family. No more handouts."

"You do what you need to, Dad, but I'm building something here, and it's my passion. You of all people should understand this type of ambition. The reality is that you never once asked what I wanted."

"This isn't a fairytale. We do what is expected of us, as did my father and grandfather. Mark my words, Harrison, you'll be begging me to take you back. In the meantime, I expect to see you at Christmas. You will not disappoint your mother."

"Sounds like the perfect family gathering."

"Don't be smart with me, Harrison. This is all your doing. It can be reversed once you realize that your little hobby isn't going to amount to anything."

"Great pep talk, Dad. My little hobby is making me a lot of money, so your demeaning rhetoric isn't going to change my mind."

I hear a click, which means dear old Dad is finished with the conversation, and he's practically finished with me, too.

Fast-forward to a year later when my grandfather dies and leaves half of his estate to me. My mother is an only child, which resulted in me being the golden grandchild. He despised my father and was one of my biggest cheerleaders. You can only imagine how my father seethed upon finding out that little tidbit of information. I thought he might have a stroke, he was so angry. It was as though he finally realized that I would never come back.

On occasion, I call my mother. Despite her usually siding with my father on most everything, she does love me in her own way. My parents are not warm people. I wish they had other children so I wouldn't be the main focus.

Nina

I feel like I'm heading toward my execution as I trudge toward the line to board my flight to West Virginia. When I come home, I'm looked at as a traitor. The whole town is oblivious to the reality that there's a world out there waiting to be explored. Or maybe they're not oblivious, and they're scared of it, which makes me the enemy. Whatever. I mean, Cassie and Marley seem happy living their lives there. Maybe it's me. Maybe I was destined to make my mark on the world. If I had stayed in that town, I would have suffocated. No, I'm happy. Really, really happy. It's as though I'm trying to give myself a pep talk into believing that statement.

Lillie might be right. A few days with Grammy will give me a bit of a reprieve. I miss her and I need to do a better job of showing her how much she means to me. After all, she isn't getting any younger and she is my everything.

My train of thought is interrupted by a very familiar scent. Don't judge me. I can't help but delight in Harrison's masculine cologne. Of course he's on this flight. I bet my former friend Addie gave him my flight information. I bet she and Jameson are laughing right now. It's like they're conspiring against me. Sprinkle Lillie in the mix and I have officially lost any choice I have in my life.

"Are you going to ignore me the whole flight?"

Damn it. Why are my earbuds in my purse?

"Oh, hello, Harrison. Are you on this flight?"

I mentally hit myself in the head with my dumb inquiry.

He chuckles, which makes me turn around to glare at him.

"Why so gloomy, Nina? You get to see Grammy and attend your high school reunion. It's going to be epic."

"The Grammy part is the only bonus. I would rather poke out my eyeballs than commune with those petulant morons."

"Gee, Nina, if I didn't know any better, I would think you're angry about your high school experience."

He's teasing, which makes me more anxious by the moment. Doesn't he have a clue that he's a big part of the dismal experience I had? If he doesn't know, that makes me hate him even more. I can't wait to sit my ass in first class, take a Xanax, and have some champagne. Yes, I realize that mixing those isn't advisable, but I don't really give a shit at this point.

I simply ignore Harrison.

The line starts to move, and I proceed through the doorway of the plane, greet the crew with a smile, and find my seat. The smooth leather soothes me as I settle in my seat and close my eyes. I turn to my seat mate, who has just put his carry-on in the overhead bin and am accosted by some familiar dimples. As Addie would say, *Fuck. My. Life.*

My smile simmers down, and I open my purse to fish out my Xanax. I hear a *tsk.*

"What?" I grit my teeth.

"Well, relying on prescription drugs to alleviate anxiety isn't healthy. For me, meditation is the root of relief. If you want me to, I can show you right now."

I glower at him, pop my Xanax—without any liquid, mind you—and eventually, my little friend travels down my throat. Relieved I didn't choke, I smile at him and say, "No thank you. I'm delighted with my happy pill."

"Suit yourself." He shrugs and puts in his earbuds. I can only assume he's deep in the throes of some "ohms" or perhaps the sound of trickling water. *Don't think of trickling water, Nina, or you'll have to pee, which means climbing over Harrison. Nope. No peeing on this flight of four hours and five minutes.* I can wait until we land in Huntington, West Virginia, where I will sprint to the restroom. That's my plan. Run to the restroom. Run to the car rental place and lose him. It's like I'm on *The Amazing Race: Solo Edition.* If there was a solo edition. Jesus, I need to get out of this headspace pronto. Thank God my happy pill has begun working its magic.

Nina

As soon as we touch down, I am poised to get the hell away from Harrison. I look forward to the solitude of driving alone to the delightful town of Conway, West Virginia, where hope dies if you stay there. Okay, that might be a little dramatic. Anyway, I have a playlist ready for my three-hour drive, and the alone time will help me get into a better mind space.

As we deplane, my view is Harrison's ass. It's a mighty fine one, I might add. What? Just because he grates on my nerves and I have unresolved issues with him, it doesn't mean I can't admire an excellent work of art. Yum.

"What did you say?" He turns around to look at me.

"I didn't say anything."

"It sounded like you said yum."

"I've got to pee," I blurt.

I swear I'm not normally awkward or unsure of myself, but hell if Harrison doesn't bring out the worst in me.

He laughs and says, "Well, let's find you a bathroom before we head to the rental car kiosk."

"You can go ahead. I'm sure we'll run into each other while we're in town. After all, the place is tiny."

"Oh, I guess Lillie didn't tell you. She cancelled your rental after I chatted with her. I mean, it's silly to have two cars when we're going to the same place. Go ahead to the restroom, I'll wait right here." His grin is grating on my nerves. I don't think I brought enough Xanax. I glare at him, plotting how I'm going to fire Lillie. Kidding. I would never fire her. I adore her even though she is a meddling hag. Returning from the bathroom, I reluctantly walk with Harrison to baggage claim, where my three bags make a prompt appearance.

"Are you moving here? I mean, Jesus, Nina, you really don't need three large pieces of luggage. I didn't rent a U-Haul," he teases.

"First of all, a woman needs options. I have no idea what the weather will be. And second of all, I might have a shoe addiction." I shrug. We head to the rental car kiosk as Harrison, being a gentleman, helps me drag my closet, aka my necessities. I might have overpacked. My insecurities are heightened going home, so it is entirely possible that I threw all my designer duds and fancy shoes into my bags to show off to the naysayers. To the ones who thought I was underwhelming. Those who made me feel less than.

I need to call my therapist.

Harrison

We spend the next hour in silence. Periodically, I glance at her. Her lips are pursed, and her face is pinched. I know coming home is painful, and I'm very aware that I caused a great deal of her pain. Coming home for me isn't much better, being the black sheep because of my unwillingness to bow down to my father's wishes to carry on the family legacy. To stay in this godforsaken town and run his empire. To me, that always sounded stifling. So now my cousin Robert is the prodigal son. The one who gets my father's admiration. I'm extremely successful, but that's not enough for Daddy dearest. He wanted me under his thumb.

When I left for college, I pledged that I would break away from his control. After what happened with Nina and prom, I knew that was just the beginning of what was to come. I needed to stand up for what I wanted instead of what I was *told* I wanted. His last words to me were, "You have always been such a disappointment," and we haven't spoken in over fifteen years since. Conversations with my mother are limited to the gossip of the rich. Shallow. Empty. Those are the words to describe my relationship with my family.

"You look constipated, Harrison." Jarred out of my thoughts, I shake my head.

"Just thinking."

"Well, your face looks all tense. If I didn't know any better, I would think you're dreading coming home just as much as I am."

"Honestly, I am. My father and I haven't spoken in over a decade, and I don't talk to my mother much." I grimace at my transparency.

"Oh. I had no idea. I thought you all were thick as thieves. You know, thinking of all the ways to make other people suffer." She shrugs as if that made any sense. As if we really sat around plotting other people's demises.

"Well, that may be what *they* do, but when I left for college, I walked away from my father's predetermined life for me. That put a wedge in our relationship. He can't seem to give me any credit for the success I've earned."

She pauses. I know she isn't used to my honesty. We spar. That's our dynamic, but her face softens, and she turns toward me.

"Maybe he can't tell you he's proud because he's hurt that you dismissed his desire to have you take over his company."

She renders me speechless, which has never happened before. I ponder her words. My father isn't one to indulge in sharing. We are not a warm family, but maybe deep down there's some truth to what Nina is saying.

"Wow. You should have gone into counseling. That was profound and insightful. You could be right, but my father's cold demeanor and all our previous interactions dictate a different scenario. He isn't capable of anything close to real feelings or deep conversation."

"I'm not all that wise. Years of therapy have given me some insight. I just think that while you're here, it might be time to address your relationship with your family. Not that it's any of my business. I'm working on not having any regrets with the people in my own life."

I hear the word "regret" and instantly go down the rabbit hole.

"Nina, I have regrets about our relationship. I know it's a long time coming, but I'm so sorry for what happened at prom. It wasn't right—I knew it then and I still know it. I've always regretted it. Words can't soothe the pain my actions caused, but that's all I can offer you. I want to move forward and be friends."

Move forward. We don't have just prom to work through. There are some situations that we need to address, but now is not the time—her grammy's house is coming into view. She's silent as I stop the car. She reaches for the door handle, and I put my hand on her arm.

"Are you going to respond to my apology?"

She doesn't look at me when she says, "I appreciate your honesty. Really, I do. It's just that what happened that night has affected every relationship I've had and has diminished my trust in people. Let me process your words. It was a lot to hear."

"Fair enough." The words tumble out, but I really don't mean them. I want this resolved. I want a place in her life, even if it is just a friendship. She means something to me, and that's rare since I was taught not to dive deep into relationships, but now I understand how profoundly my actions affected her life and it wounds me. She's not just holding a grudge, she's holding on to hurt. I should have made amends before now, but the timing hasn't always been perfect. Besides, her being trapped in a car with me was ideal; experience dictates she's a runner.

I get out of the car and retrieve her luggage. Grammy comes out of the house and her face lights up when she lays her eyes on Nina. Nina's expression softens, her eyes wet with tears, as she turns to me and says, "Thanks for the ride, Harrison. See you around."

Nina

I'm overwhelmed by the conversation I had with Harrison. Jesus, I can't believe how honest he was, and the admission of regret as to what happened at prom deflated my anger. My overthinking can wait as I embrace Grammy. She smells like home. I inhale the lavender scent and smile as I melt into her hug. She is my guiding light, and I'm so grateful for her.

"Good God, girl! I need to fatten you up. Are you still eating that kale crap?"

"It's not crap, Grammy. It's healthy and I like it." I sound a tad defensive, but come on, she's attacking kale for God's sake.

"Well, there is no kale in this house. Only good old comfort food." She looks over my shoulder and sees Harrison struggling with my luggage. She walks over to him, her arms open wide to embrace him. What the actual fuck? I thought she was on Team Nina.

"Look at you, Harrison. Aren't you a hottie!" She whistles. Grammy is one big flirt.

Harrison blushes and I simply close my eyes and shake my head. Grammy has never had a filter.

He walks into her embrace and says, "You're still as beautiful as ever. Haven't aged a bit."

"Aren't you a sweet talker. Well, thank you for getting my girl home safely. Do you want to stay for dinner?"

No, no, no! Ugh. I can't believe she's inviting him for dinner after I was stuck with him all day, and we just had that emotionally charged conversation. I just want to take off my bra and get comfortable.

"You are sweet to offer, but I'm having dinner with my family tonight. Before I head back to New York, I would love to have dinner with you all though."

"Harrison, you are always welcome." She grins at him and bats her eyelashes. What the hell is happening? I'm beyond curious as to what has transformed her attitude toward him.

He hugs her again, grabs my luggage and puts it inside the front door.

"Nina, do you want me to put these in your room?"

"No thank you. I can manage on my own. Been doing it long enough." My tone is clipped, and I instantly cringe at myself. Why did I say that? It sounds like an accusation and an admission all at once.

"Of course. You're an independent woman. Well, I will leave you in the capable hands of your grammy." He turns and walks out the door. I want to call him back and apologize, but I remain quiet. Irritated with myself, I watch as his car disappears into the night.

Nina

The house is filled with the familiar homey smells of food laden with calories. Good thing I brought my expandable relaxed yoga pants. Don't grimace at me. Every woman has a pair. They're usually for when your monthly friend visits, but I bring them to Grammy's because she will watch me until I eat every morsel of her delicious, carb-filled dishes. Seriously, I gain at least ten pounds visiting. My skinny jeans scream, "Why?" when I try to put them on after days of eating her mouthwatering concoctions.

"Nina, you better spill." I watch as she layers my plate with more food than anyone could eat in a sitting: fried chicken, green beans that have been simmering for a couple of hours with bacon, her five-cheese macaroni and cheese, along with two biscuits—the best buttermilk biscuits I've ever tasted. We sit down together at the kitchen table.

"About what? Do you want to hear about work? Addie? My new clients are pretty interesting. I could go on about the new organic kale I found at the farmers' market near my apartment." I smirk.

"Girly, you know exactly what I'm talking about. You had hours with Harrison, and that boy looks at you like you're his last meal."

I take a breath and exhale. She will not let this go. She's relentless when fishing for information. This formidable woman should have been in the CIA because people cave in her presence.

"We just happened to be on the same flight, same row of seats, and shared the rental car to get here."

She rolls her eyes at me. Wow, the older she gets, the sassier she becomes.

"Nina, you may have business smarts, but your romance skills are lacking. I already know something happened since you looked so confused when you got out of his car. You might as well tell me why."

She stares at me expectantly. What am I supposed to do, lie to her? I cave.

I tell her about the apology and the admission of his difficult relationship with his family. I share that I told him about how his actions had a domino effect into every relationship I've ever had. I tell her how wounded he looked with that confession. What I don't say is that *I'm* the one who has been wounded, and as much as I appreciate his very late apology, he probably only did it to make things less awkward between us. I resent that.

"So that's it? You simply left it?"

"What was I supposed to do? Just say, 'Sure, I forgive you, everything's fine' after all this time? I mean, I guess we could try being friends—that's the best I could do. Our best friends are getting married, and we're both in the wedding. It seems like a natural progression." I shrug.

"My sweet, naïve, closed-off Nina. You're oblivious to the torch he holds for you. He looks at you like you're the sun and the moon. For God's sake, get your head out of your ass."

Did my grammy just accuse me of having my head up my ass? Are you kidding me right now?

"Look, I know you love those romance novels, but he doesn't look at me like that. He tolerates me at best, and sometimes I hate him—most of the time, actually—so I don't see much more happening."

Grammy touches my hand. "There is a fine line between love and hate, Nina. You're not in high school anymore. What happened was unfortunate, but you have allowed it to define you. I know you think you're strong because of all you've accomplished, and yes, all of that is amazing and wonderful. But true strength is in forgiveness."

With that, she gets up from the table and starts cleaning up the kitchen while I wallow in my own thoughts.

Harrison

I pull the rental car into the circular driveway in front of the mansion where my parents live. I grew up here, but I never called it home. Home is warm. Full of love. Home is where Nina grew up. *Nina*. She's all I've thought about since our conversation. Her confession about how my actions affected her whole life really made me think … and regret. And here I thought she was just playing aloof and hard to get. Jesus. I am such a fucking asshole.

I reluctantly get out of the car and retrieve my luggage from the trunk. I chuckle when I see that one of her smaller suitcases has been left, and I realize that now I have an excuse to see her. That made my heart skip a little, or maybe that was a heart palpitation in preparation for being with my family.

I close the trunk and head to the massive front door. Do I ring the bell? I have a key, assuming they haven't changed the locks. I can't even remember how long it has been since I graced this place with my presence. As I contemplate my choices, the door opens and I'm greeted by Gerald, their butler. Gerald has been employed by my family since I was old enough to remember. He looks the same, but he must be close to seventy—tall and distinguished-looking, with salt and pepper streaking his black hair. His serious deportment might intimidate most people, but underneath he's a big softie.

"Mr. Harrison, welcome home!" He bows a little bit. I laugh.

"Oh, come on, Gerry! Let's hug it out." He grimaces when I call him Gerry, however, he honors my request by returning my embrace. He chuckles as I release him.

"Mr. Harrison, it is good to see you. It's been a while. I know your parents will be pleased you're home."

"There's no need to lie to me The truth is that you're the only one I'm happy to see. Where are the parental units? I assume in the lounge enjoying their cocktails?" I move my bags into the foyer.

He shakes his head, a slight smile dancing on his lips.

"Sir, they're in the lounge awaiting your presence. Dinner will be served promptly at seven."

"Of course. That leaves me with an hour to listen to my father berate me for my life choices. Well, at least there's bourbon."

He nods and leads the way. Yes, I grew up in a pretentious home where guests were announced before they entered a room. Guess who the guest is in this scenario? Bingo. Moi.

"May I announce the arrival of Mr. Harrison."

I walk into the room and am greeted by the shifty eyes of my high school ex-girlfriend, Melanie Hart, and her equally shady parents, Bunny and Gabe Hart, looking awfully cozy with my parents. My father smirks while my mother tries to smile, but the amount of Botox pumped into her face makes that difficult. Melanie launches herself on me.

"Oh, Harrison, I am positively thrilled you're home! Handsome as ever."

She wraps me in a tight hug, so I return it to avoid being totally rude. My arms go limp around her. I give her a pat on her back, trying to get her to stop. The four sets of eyes are watching our interaction carefully. I feel the warning bells. Red flags waving. I feel like my best course of action would be to run, but something has glued me to the floor. Melanie is gorgeous. Perfectly outfitted in a linen sheath dress that accentuates her figure. Her porcelain skin is painted in makeup—too much, if you ask me. Her wavy blond hair settles on her shoulders. I used to find her irresistible. She was my first everything until she cheated on me during our junior year. But now when I look at her, I feel nothing.

She isn't Nina.

Woah. Where the fuck did that come from? I shake away the thought as I try to focus on the scene before me.

"Mother." I kiss the cheek she offers me. Bitsy looks the same. Designer dress accented with pearls. Minimal makeup, with her blond hair in a chiffon twist. Her tall, model-like figure is maintained by the eating disorder she tries to hide, but I know. I have always known. Living with my mother has affected me in different ways.

"Father." I shake his hand. His hair is gray now, but his chiseled features and muscular frame have not changed with time. Our height is the same at six feet, and that's the *only* way in which we see eye to eye. I cock my head as a subtle question of, "What are you up to, old man?" He stares me down as if to challenge me. I release his hand and turn to our other guests.

"Bunny, don't you look lovely. You haven't aged a bit." I give her that stupid kiss on each cheek. Manners and appearances are of the utmost importance.

"Gabe, hope you're well. It's good to see you." I shake his limp hand and zero in on my only friend in the room: bourbon. All of this is one big lie, of course. It's never good to see any of these people.

I head to the bar and pour myself a double. Turning to my audience, I say, "Well, I had no idea that you were having a dinner party. To what do I owe the pleasure?"

At that moment, Melanie latches on to my arm and says, "Oh Harrison, we have the best news! It's about our future. The future of Mr. and Mrs. Harrison McCall."

Harrison

"What the fuck did you just say to me?" I rip my arm away from her and Melanie gasps.

I hear a *tsk* coming from my mother. "Language, Harrison."

"Well, fortunately, Mother, I am a grown man who's not under your thumb, so I can say *fuck* all I want. In fact, that is the perfect word for this particular situation." I stare at my father. "Explain."

He clears his throat. "You're getting to the age where your man-whoring ways are not a good representation of our family. A union between you and Melanie could be quite lucrative. Gabe wants to retire, so by your marriage to Melanie, we could merge the companies and create an empire." My father's eyes glimmer with greed. My eyes glimmer with anger. He's been arranging my life all this time. They've all talked about this and made decisions about my whole future without me. After all I've done and all I've said about this, they're still acting like I'm a plaything.

I throw the glass of bourbon against the wall. As the crystal shatters, there is a collective gasp. I regret the action. Not because I threw the glass, but because I wasted my liquid courage when I reacted.

"Have we stepped back in time to when arranged marriages were trendy?" I rage. "Not playing your game. I have a successful company that's very lucrative. I not only don't need you, I don't want you in my life. It was a mistake to come here, and one that will *not* be made again. I'm out of here."

My father's voice bellows, "Harrison, you will not leave, and you will participate. You see, I have eyes and ears everywhere. I know you have a soft spot for little Nina, and if you want her business to continue to succeed, you *will* participate."

"What are you talking about, old man?" We are eye to eye, toe to toe. The urge to punch him is strong, but instead I clench my fist at my side.

"Nina has some secrets. Some things that if they were to get out, well, let's just say her clients would not look at her the same way. I can ruin her. This way it's a win-win for everyone. Melanie is excited to move to New York with you, and with our merger, we'll all be swimming in money and power."

Delusional must be the theme for the evening.

"I knew I shouldn't have come. What secrets are you talking about? I bet I already know them anyway." That's a lie. I don't know of any secrets at all, but I'm hoping my bluff will make him back down. Besides, Nina doesn't have anything hidden. Does she? Doubt blankets my thoughts. I need to call Jameson. He was able to uncover the shit show regarding the reappearance of Addie's long-lost father, who turned out to be a fraud, only to reveal that her biological father is none other than Senator Wendell Brooks. If he could do all that, he can help me here.

"Oh, son, we can't lay our cards on the table just yet. But soon. Very soon. In the meantime, Gertrude has prepared an amazing meal. Let's proceed to the dining room."

"Forget it. I've lost my appetite." I turn to leave, and I hear Melanie squeak, "Where are you going?" while my father says, "We are not done by any stretch of the imagination."

I head out the door, get in my car, and dial my best friend's number. It goes to voicemail and I leave a simple message: "I need your help."

 Nina

I f there is a real medical condition called "food coma," I have it. I ate my weight in carb- loaded food to appease my grammy. Oh, who am I kidding, this was my life before I discovered a healthier way of eating. I feel better when I'm not indulging. But right now, I need a blanket, a pillow, and some peace and quiet on the couch.

As I close my eyes to embrace my comatose state, my zen is interrupted by two loud interlopers. Ugh. I know those voices.

"Oh no you don't. There will be no sleeping. You barely visit, and when you do, you breeze through without us going out and painting the town."

I open one eye to stare at my closest friends growing up. Marley reminds me of Addie except, if you can believe it, she's even more boisterous and pushy. Her long, chestnut hair is in a high ponytail, while her toned legs are on display with her extremely short minidress. Cassie is a little quieter and blossomed into this beautiful, willowy woman. Her short hair is slicked back, making her hazel eyes pop. Her skinny jeans are complemented by a chic, sparkly halter top. Both are grinning at me.

In high school, we were not attractive. We were labeled as geeks, but look at us now. We have arrived. All three of us are successful businesswomen. The two of them own this adorable clothing boutique in town that caters to the big spenders. In fact, I need to make a note to stop in while I'm here. I even brought an extra suitcase, just in case I found some new clothes. A girl can never have too many choices in attire.

Back to the two standing before me. My stop for the evening is this couch, but I know they want to hit the only bar in town, The Watering Hole.

After the initial hugging and squealing, which resulted in the unfortunate action of me actually standing up, the manipulation begins.

"Paint the town red? You realize that would take all of five minutes. Let's watch a movie instead. Grammy has peach cobbler left over." I plop back onto the couch and wiggle my eyebrows, hoping that will be enough to entice them.

"Nope. Get your ass up. We're going out and you're going to like it, but first we need to glam you up. Surely you have some fashionable clothes from snooty New York." Marley laughs because I hardly own anything but fashionable clothes. "You have fifteen minutes."

"I can't. I hardly spend any time with Grammy, and this is our time together."

"Girl, don't use me as an excuse. Go have some fun. I'm going to bed, anyway."

Jesus, she has eagle ears. I huff and throw my cozy blanket off. I hug them again and say, "I hate you both." They giggle and Marley slaps my ass.

"You're down to fourteen minutes."

I hustle upstairs and get ready, picking out some black skinny jeans and pairing them with an off-the-shoulder top. Put on some subtle makeup. Brush my hair and let it lay on my shoulders. I give myself a once-over in the mirror and deeply realize that the girl looking back at me is no longer that timid teenager, not even in her hometown. I'm a strong, independent woman who is successful. I gather my clutch with my phone, lip gloss, credit card, and ID, and head downstairs to my very impatient and annoying friends.

"Happy now?" I ask as I meet them at the front door.

"Well, I was hoping you would wear a tiny dress that showed more skin, but this will do. You're hot wearing just about anything, and it is so unfair." Marley scoffs.

"Ladies, I think we all are extremely hot. Seriously."

"Let's go. We can walk and you can fill us in on your travel adventures with Harrison." Cassie wiggles her eyebrows at me.

These two are killing me.

Making our way out onto the sidewalk, we start toward the bar. "Is that the gossip floating around town? Things have definitely not changed. There isn't anything to tell. We ended up on the same flight and were seat mates. Then we shared a rental car because he'd already arranged for it with my assistant. On the way, he apologized for what he did at prom and dropped me off at Grammy's. That's it."

I realize that they stopped. I turn around and say, "What? Why did you stop?"

Both of their mouths are hanging open, and after several seconds of silence, Marley says, "He apologized? Harrison McCall? The man you see a lot in New York waited until now to actually make amends to you after all these years?"

"Yep." I pop the P for affect.

"Well, this calls for tequila, which is your truth serum, my friend."

She finally starts walking again and brushes past me, and I have no choice but to follow. We walk into the bar only to come face-to-face with Harrison himself. Well, hell.

Harrison

After I checked into the bed and breakfast, I felt I deserved to get drunk. That fucked-up interaction with my parents and Melanie left me spinning, and anyway, I've got to waste some time before I head back, preferably when they're asleep, to get my bags. You see, I left them in the foyer like an idiot.

I find a seat at the bar and wait for Marty, the owner of The Watering Hole, to notice me. If you're expecting glamorous, think again. The floors are worn, with a slight stickiness to them. Marty probably dims the lights on purpose so you can't see the décor, which, by the way, hasn't changed in decades. It's like dark wood threw up everywhere. The only ambience worth mentioning is the jukebox in the corner.

"Well, well, well, what brings big-shot Harrison back to our humble town?"

I notice that he doesn't refer to this town as my home.

"Hey, Marty. Good to see you. Give me a double of your best bourbon."

"You fancy New Yorkers, always ordering the expensive stuff."

"Marty, you know who my parents are, right? It's got nothing to do with New York. It's my lineage." I chuckle and he smirks.

"Well, a double tells me you got problems. Tell old Marty what ails you."

"Nope. Small town, big ears, and even bigger mouths. In New York, I could tell the bartender anything and nobody gives a shit. Here, my lips are sealed."

"We'll see how sealed they are after a few of these." He smirks and pours me a double.

I take a drink, relishing the amber liquid as it burns my throat. Closing my eyes, I exhale and try to shake the events of the day. I feel the tension escape my body and I open my eyes, only to see Nina walking in with her best friends from high school, Marley and Cassie. Jesus, why is it that she literally takes my breath away every time I see her? I was trying to escape, but I suppose that concept doesn't apply in a small town. Maybe a little antagonizing will make me feel better.

"Stalking me, Bryant?" I grin at her while I hug her friends.

"Hardly. It isn't like there's anywhere else to go. Besides, maybe you're stalking me." There's a sparkle in her eye that I notice before it extinguishes. Before it's shadowed by uncertainty and distrust. I did that to her.

"Ladies, allow me to buy you a drink." Both Marley and Cassie settle for white wine while Nina orders bourbon, neat. Not surprised at all. It's like we're made for each other. After our conversation, I thought we were moving forward, but now with my parents and their ridiculous demands, I feel like I need to keep her at arm's length. At least until I chat with Jameson. Maybe the alcohol will loosen fair Nina's lips and I can find out what my family thinks is so damaging. What is Nina hiding?

"Why are you staring at me?" Her eyes narrow. Her lips purse. God, she is stunning even when her buttons are pushed.

"Just your beauty."

"Save those empty pickup lines for your harem."

"You think I have a harem? Well, Nina, I didn't think you noticed. Are you jealous?" I smirk.

"Hardly. It's impossible not to notice the revolving door."

Someone behind us clears their throat, and before I know it, there are several sets of eyes on us, enjoying the show. I constantly forget that this is a small town, and everyone is always watching everyone else. Cassie laughs.

"Doesn't seem like much has changed," Marley says. "Maybe you all need to just fuck each other and get it out of your system." She takes a drink of her wine, her eyes never leaving our faces.

Nina reddens and I simply focus on my drink. We chartered that unknown territory once and have avoided discussing it since. But one time with Nina will never be enough. Addie and Jameson have no idea, even though it happened under their noses in Italy after they announced their engagement.

"I feel like we're missing something. I think tequila shots are in order, Marley. That will get our beautiful Nina to spill," Cassie says with a glimmer of mischief in her eyes.

As I'm reminiscing in my head about the best night of my life, the door to the bar opens, and in walks Melanie. Her eyes are laser-focused on me, stalking me like I'm her prey. I don't think there's enough alcohol for this.

Nina

I'm still recovering from Marley's obnoxious comment when Melanie walks into the bar, looking as bitchy as ever. I chug my bourbon—because I'm classy like that—and order another one. Melanie is one of those people you hope has changed since high school but hasn't matured beyond a seventeen-year-old entitled hag. Put me back in my New York City element and I am fierce. But here in this tiny little town, I revert to an insecure teenage girl. Intimidated.

Buck up, Nina. You are powerful. You are strong. You are a force.

I need Aibileen Clark to tell me, "You is kind. You is smart. You is important." That woman could heal anyone's soul.

I'm in my own world when I hear Melanie's screeching voice say, "Well, well, well, look who's here to grace us with her presence. It's so cute you went all the way to New York City just to get away from all the humiliation."

I turn to face her and take in her appearance. She hasn't changed much. Her blond hair cascades down her back, and she's dressed head to toe in designer wear. Her plunging neckline shows off her girls in all their glory. Her shapely body fills out her skinny jeans with ease.

I wish the years had been unkind and she had become an ugly troll. Petty? Yes, but I can't help being a little vindictive.

"Melanie, you're looking well. So good to see you." The bile is inching up my throat, but I can be the bigger person. I work with temperamental writers. I negotiate contracts. I work in a man's world. I can deal with this vile bitch.

"I was so surprised to see you on the reunion list as a 'yes.' I just couldn't believe it. I mean, if it were me, I would never show my face again."

She's baiting me. And old me would have slinked away. But this is the new me. I'm a hardened New Yorker that spits out cocky businessmen for a hobby.

"I suppose that's the difference between you and me. That was high school. We're adults now, so I really don't see the point in rehashing the past. I guess if that's all you have, I understand a little better. But I've grown up since high school. I'm a successful businesswoman. I don't have time for bitches."

Melanie gasps. Marley grins and Cassie holds up her glass as if she were toasting me. And Harrison, he has a look of pride on his face. That felt amazing.

I slam back the last of my bourbon. Not going to lie, I'm shaking, but I cover it by turning my attention to my two friends, and I try not to make eye contact with Harrison.

"You might think you won, Ms. Nobody, but *I* am the winner, and I'll tell you why. I'm set to be Mrs. Harrison McCall. Isn't that right, Harrison?" She raises her eyebrow at him. I turn and look at him. What the actual fuck? He looks at me. I can't read his expression, but before he opens his mouth, I turn back to Melanie.

"Well, I can't think of two people who deserve each other more." I get up and say my goodbyes to Marley and Cassie, who have apparently been stunned into silence.

Dramatic exit complete. I applaud myself and my badassness. Then I realize I forgot my purse. Fuck. My. Life.

Harrison

Nina's verbal smackdown of Melanie makes me want her even more. She's a formidable opponent and Melanie is no match. Nina's expression is blanketed in confusion and hurt. I desperately want to explain the whole bizarre setup my father has instituted. I want to tell her that Melanie is nothing to me, but Nina storms out before I can make a show of telling her the truth. Out of the corner of my eye, I spot her purse still sitting on the bar. She must have forgotten it. I pick it up, say my goodbyes to Cassie and Marley, who are now glaring at me, and head to the door, pushing past Melanie. Melanie grabs my arm and whispers into my ear, "Daddy says we should be dating and making public appearances for our new relationship." Her eyes fill with lust.

"Funny story, Melanie—I haven't agreed to any of that nonsense. We aren't anything and we never will be. Your father may control your life, but he doesn't and he never will control mine."

She gasps and sputters, reminding me of my old dirt bike when I would first fire it up. I walk out the door and find Nina pacing back and forth, muttering to herself about how she couldn't possibly go back in there.

"Did you forget something?" I dangle her purse in front of her with a big grin on my face.

"Oh thank God. I was wondering how I was going to walk in there and face Satan's spawn after my dramatic exit. Of all the times to be considerate and leave my phone in my purse. I've learned my lesson there."

"Are you planning on more verbal smackdowns in the future? I personally enjoyed that one very much."

"You did? I didn't want to be nasty, but seriously, we're old enough to move on from all the emotional angst from high school."

"Does that mean you forgive me for what I did that night? I had no idea what my parents planned for prom. I know I hurt you, and I will hold that guilt the rest of my life, but that moment was the catalyst to breaking free from their hold and to finally find my voice."

Nina sighs. "I suppose I understand that it was out of your control. You were young and impressionable. I get it, but … there's still that part of me that wishes you'd chosen me." Her eyes glisten with unshed tears.

I move closer to her. Slowly, since she's a flight risk, and grab her hand. "You have no idea how much I wish I had done everything differently that night." We stand there hand in hand, and I wish our past had not hurt her so badly.

Then a switch inside her seems to flip, and she takes her hand back as if it were on fire.

"Seems congratulations are in order. I had no idea that you and Melanie were close, but I guess we don't share a lot about our lives unless it involves Addie and Jameson. Tell me, were you with her while we were in Italy?"

Before I can tell her that this is just a game my dad is playing, the sound of a throat clearing loudly comes from behind us. Nina's face whitens. I turn to see who has shattered the moment and am met with Melanie's angry eyes. I turn back to see Nina walking away.

Harrison

If Melanie weren't such a bitch, she would be gorgeous, but her ugly, colorless personality can't help but shine through. She is one dimensional. It's all about what can best serve her agenda, and unfortunately, right now that's me. Why did I even bother coming back here?

"Honey buns, Daddy was so excited when you asked me out, and yet I feel a little lonely in there." She swaggers over to me and grabs my arm possessively.

I turn to look at her and say, "We are not together. We will never be together. I just told you that. What didn't you understand?"

"You're just in a bad mood. We were so good together in high school, don't you remember? And this makes Daddy happy. Don't you care about your little friend enough to make this work?" She smirks.

I want to explain to Nina, but I can't detach myself fast enough from Melanie, and all I see is Nina's fast stride as she stalks down the street. Everything we shared in Italy when Addie and Jameson got engaged evaporated the moment we landed on American soil. And now, being back in this godforsaken town is just another reminder of her distrust in me. I close my eyes and take a deep breath.

"Let me be clear. I will not be participating in this little scheme that our families have concocted."

"It's funny that you think you have a choice. I never have, and your parents aren't too different from mine. They let you have your fun for a while, but now it's time to fulfill your father's plans for us. Don't forget, *I'm* the one who's been stuck here waiting for *you*. Besides, I've always wanted to live in New York and spend my days shopping, lunching, and going to spas."

"Isn't that basically what you do now? Sucking the life out of everyone you touch. Spending money that isn't yours and acting as if you're the center of the universe," I bark.

She laughs at me. Most women would cry or maybe look hurt, but she is fucking laughing at me.

"When did you get so angry? Maybe you need me to loosen you up. We used to be so good together." She puts her hand on my chest. I roll my eyes.

"I would have fucked anything when I was seventeen. You were one of many. Don't flatter yourself into thinking you were special."

I leave her as she begins to have what can only be described as a tantrum, stomping her feet and screaming incoherently at me. Jesus.

I head back to my parents' home to retrieve my luggage since I stormed out without it. My phone rings, and I see it's Jameson.

"Hey," I say weakly.

"Well, hello. Not to be an asshole, but you sound pathetic."

Damn he's good.

See, even he can hear it through the phone. I feel trapped. I tell him about the run-in with my father and his ultimatum.

"You aren't buying into that bullshit, are you? Nina has nothing to hide that would ruin her. She's the epitome of an honest businesswoman, and she did that all by herself."

"I know that, but I need to cover all of my bases. Can you get your friend, Grady, to do some research into my family and Nina? I hate to investigate her, but I need to protect her."

Grady works with Jameson and helped uncover the blackmailing scheme Addie's cousin-in-law, Dorothy, set into motion. She partnered up with Addie's fake father before it became clear that former Senator Wendell Brooks is Owen's and her real father. Products of a long affair with their mother. It was a mess, but Dorothy ended up in prison, and Addie and Owen are building a relationship with the former senator. The bonus is that Jameson found Addie. She grounds him and makes him less broody, and I'll always be grateful for that.

"Are you sure you want to go this route? You could always ask Nina directly."

"I could, but our relationship is complicated. She tolerates me on a good day. Look, I just think this is the only way." I realize that I'm not totally justified in taking this step, but I can't exactly say, "Hey, Nina, my father has some kind of blackmail on you. Care to tell me what it is?"

Jameson sighs. "Look, you care about Nina, and I get that in order to keep her safe, this is what you feel you have to do. I did the same thing to Addie and I would do it all over again for her. That's what you do for the people you love. But remember that I almost lost her when I wasn't honest. Keep that in mind before you make this decision."

Love. Who the hell mentioned love? My stomach clenches.

"Man, I'm not in love. I just don't want to hurt her any more than I already have. After all these years, I finally have a slim shot at making things right with her. I can't mess that up now. I care about her, yeah, but I'm not in love with her."

The fucker laughs. "Keep telling yourself that. This is literally what happened with Addie and me, and now I'm planning a wedding. Well, she's planning a wedding. I just have to show up. I have no idea what the story is between the two of you. I just hope that you'll share it when the time is right. All I know is that there's something more there. Just be careful you don't fuck it up."

"Wow, that was some solid Oprah advice. Look, you and Addie are different. Nina and I will never get to that point. She needs someone who won't cause her heartache."

"Well, then she needs to marry a unicorn, because you can't escape hurting those you love. It's called being human."

"Shit, when did you get so soft?"

"When I fell in love, asshole. Call me if you need anything else or if you want to talk about your feelings." He snickers.

"Last I looked, I haven't grown a vagina."

He laughs. I need to stop being such excellent entertainment for my friend.

"Email me the information you want Grady to look into and I'll get the ball rolling."

"Thanks, man. Appreciate your help on this."

"I just hope you know what you're doing. Later, H."

"Me too." I end the call and shake my head. I am in deep.

Harrison

I pull up to the mausoleum that I grew up in and am pleased to find the house is dark. Like a wannabe ninja, I creep into the foyer to retrieve my bag. I'm waiting for my father to accost me, but silence is the only thing that greets me. What a sweet sound. I put my hand on the door handle to leave, and a voice reaches out from the darkness.

"Do you really think that by leaving this house, you can escape the inevitable?"

I take a breath and without turning around, say, "The only thing that's inevitable is that I won't be participating in this scheme of yours. You're no longer in control of my life."

He laughs. You know the evil laugh you hear in the movies when the bad guy thinks he's won? That is the sound that reverberates off the walls. "I am very much in control of everything, Harrison. You'd better think long and hard about that Bryant girl and how I can destroy her. What I'm going to do will make prom look like a day at an amusement park."

I hear his steps leave the room, and I'm left feeling more confused than ever. What dark secrets is Nina hiding?

Nina

There is a single light burning bright in the window as I enter Grammy's home. A slight smile tugs at my mouth. I exhale as I enter. Trying to be quiet and not wake her, I take off my heels and tiptoe to my room. The floors creak. To be honest, I'm trying to escape the inquisition until breakfast. I don't want to talk about Harrison or the appendage that was stroking his chest the last time I looked over my shoulder at him. I don't want to relive the moment we shared when he held my hand. Why does my heart continue to ache? I realize it doesn't take a genius to figure out that I'm a walking cliché. The feelings I have for Harrison are complicated. I can't seem to get over him, which means seeing him with anyone else makes my fists clench. I want to throat punch them. I can at least admit that, but honestly, I can't go there again. My heart can't take it.

I shed my clothes and put on my pajamas. If Addie saw me now, she would high-five me and laugh. While I'm always put together just so, I'm currently comfy in my Rolling Stones T-shirt and boy shorts. I miss Addie. I texted her a few minutes ago on my walk home to see if she could talk. I don't want to interrupt anything between her and Jameson. My phone pings incessantly. Cassie's and Marley's concerned messages illuminate my screen. I type out that I'm fine and I'll talk with them tomorrow. They can be as bad as Addie when it comes to fishing out information.

As I head back from my nightly skincare routine in the bathroom, I hear my phone ringing. I hope it's her. I could really use the comfort of my best friend's voice right now. I've been feeling guilty lately that she doesn't know everything about me, especially about Harrison and my history together. I'm not sure if I should tell her soon. I shut my bedroom door and look at my phone. It's her!

"Hey!" The chipper voice I use doesn't sound like me. I don't do chipper, and she can read me like a book.

"That was the lamest, fakest 'hey' I have ever heard. What the fuck is wrong and who do I need to kill?" she deadpans.

The thing about Addie is that she's my ride or die. She would help me bury a body with no questions asked. You need people like that in your life.

"Where's Jameson? Did he pass out from all the sex you're having?" I laugh at my own joke. Distraction is the new plan, because suddenly I don't really want to talk about it. Any of it.

"Stop deflecting. There's something wrong. Harrison called Jameson about you and it sounded serious, and then I got your text too. I'm worried about you. Tell me *everything*! What the hell is going on with Harrison and you?"

Why is Harrison calling Jameson about me? Did he tell him the truth about us?

I know Addie. She's not going to let this go, so I suppose it's time for the big reveal. I tell her everything, including the apology, the exchange with Melanie, and last but certainly not the least, the fact that we had sex in Italy while there to celebrate Addie and Jameson's engagement. Lots and lots of sex. Surprised? Well, I was too. But it was Italy, plus copious amounts of wine. Ugh. Then we came back to New York and I pushed him and all my feelings away. I just can't get past our past. I'm pathetic. I'm scared. He wanted more, but I just couldn't go down that road. What if we got serious and he stood me up *at our wedding*? I couldn't live through that.

When I finish, she's quiet. A quiet Addie is a scary Addie.

"Well, that is a lot of information to absorb. I mean, I'm a little hurt that you hadn't shared that with me before now. I can get past that since it sounds like you've really been hurt by Harrison's actions. I can punch him if you want. I don't care about him being best friends with the love of my life. You are my forever, girl."

I tear up. Strong, fierce Nina doesn't cry. I don't show my vulnerability because it makes me weak, but this is Addie. Before I can say anything, she continues.

"Now, tell me about the sex. Did your vajayjay sing? Mine has a playlist."

And then, I just burst out laughing because that is what Addie does for me. She knows that revealing myself to her was hard even though she is my person. She can always make me feel better.

"We're not talking about the sex. Sure, it was amazing, but we aren't going there again." I try to sound convincing.

"Uh huh, well, you sound like me denying what was going on with Jameson. Will you call me if you need me? No more secrets, Nina."

"I will, and I'm sorry that I didn't tell you everything. It's hard to talk about, and frankly, I probably need to go back to my therapist since obviously I haven't worked through this."

"Nina, you are such an incredible woman. Despite your odd obsession with kale, I think the world is much brighter with you in it. You are family, Nina. We've got your back always."

Now I'm full on crying.

"Jesus, Nina, are you crying? Can we FaceTime because I want to see if you're a pretty crier or if you look like everyone else?"

I laugh in between tears. I honor her request, because if we're going to be fully transparent, then she needs to see me messy.

Her face pops up on the screen. She's frowning.

"What the fuck are you wearing? Is that a T-shirt? How much shit do I get for wearing the exact same attire?"

"Yes, this is a T-shirt and I give you shit because you think T-shirts are appropriate clothing for all occasions." I laugh through the tears.

She scoffs. "You and George keep conspiring against me."

George is her stylist and close friend. He revamped her wardrobe even though she still hoards T-shirts and yoga pants. She still needs help dressing. A grown woman. Seriously.

"Jesus, you aren't a pretty crier. Thank God. You're all red and splotchy. Makes me feel like you aren't some sort of anomaly of perfection."

"I'm so glad my messy distress pleases you." I grin at her. Her ridiculousness is humorous.

"You might want to put some ice on your eyes. Those suckers are going to be puffy tomorrow."

She has an excellent way of helping me see my own humanness. I love her for that.

"Addie, I appreciate you more than you know."

"Of course you do. I'm a delightful ray of sunshine packaged in T-shirts and yoga pants. What's not to love? Now get some sleep. Things always look better in the morning."

"Love you."

"Love you back."

The call ends and I finally feel like I can breathe.

Nina

The night was sleepless. The tossing and turning just exacerbated my bad mood. Addie was wrong. I don't feel better. I'm back to hating Harrison. He wanted more and I couldn't move forward and now he has moved on with my nemesis. Good for them. They deserve each other.

I head to the bathroom, where I grimace at my reflection. Everything in the mirror is chaotic. My eyes are puffy, my hair looks like a rat's nest. I'm one hot mess and not in a good way. I sigh. Splashing cool water on my face feels good. I brush my teeth, change, and put my hair in a high ponytail. Maybe coffee will help me, and after that, I have a few hours of work ahead of me, regardless of my "time off." No rest for the weary, and I am especially weary today.

I head downstairs where the smell of coffee and bacon permeates the air. Don't tell Addie—it will fuel her fire of wanting me to indulge in bar food with her. Cue my shudder. Anyway, Grammy is an amazing cook, and it would be rude to not eat what she makes, right? A smile spreads across my face as I round the corner—until I hear a familiar voice. My eyes land on Harrison's delectable backside. Just because

I'm annoyed with him doesn't mean my eyes aren't sharp enough to appreciate his looks.

Grammy is laughing at something Harrison is saying, and I feel a pang of longing. I suck in a breath, exhale, and enter the kitchen.

"Good morning, Grammy." I give her a kiss on the cheek, inhaling the sweet scent of lavender. Feelings of regret plague me for not putting all my hurt behind me and visiting her more.

In passing, I mutter, "Harrison," and head to the coffeepot. I look up and my eyes meet his. He observes me in a concerned way. Nope. Not today. I will be strong.

"Everything okay?" he asks as his brow furrows.

"Everything's great. Busy day." I smile. Not a real one. Those are saved for the people I trust, and right now I don't trust him.

"Maybe we can talk today."

I tilt my head at him and say, "What exactly do we need to discuss, Harrison?"

Harrison never looks vulnerable, but I see a flash of it. I eye him.

"Let's go to lunch. There's this new spot on the outside of town that I heard is really good. We can go there to get away from any interruptions."

"Interruptions" means his girlfriend and his horrible parents. I sigh. My resolve crumbles.

"Okay." I meet his eyes.

"Great! I'll pick you up at noon." He grins at me and my heart flutters. My brain and body are definitely not on the same page.

He turns to leave, thanking Grammy for breakfast, and if I'm not mistaken, there is pep in his step. I watch him get into his car as I sip my coffee, completely lost in thought until I hear a throat clearing. My grandmother is grinning.

"Sit down and tell me everything."

Good Lord, what am I doing?

Nina

I refuse to indulge her. I won't tell her everything about Harrison. I will be strong, but I also know she's like a dog with a bone. She has always been able make me spill. I can't hide anything from her. I'm sixteen all over again.

"Grammy, I really don't want to talk about it. Suffice it to say, we're like oil and water."

"That boy loves you. He always has."

What? No, that isn't possible. Doesn't love involve trust, putting the other person first, and possibly not arguing over every little thing? No, he isn't in love with me. I could understand why she wishes he was—he treats her so well. She must think he treats me just as well, but he doesn't.

I dismiss the notion. "You have no idea what you're talking about, Grammy. We have a lot of history, mostly bad, and now we share a lot of professional clients, but that's it."

Grammy's demeanor changes as her eyes look down at her wrinkled hands. She exhales and says, "I have something to tell you. Something that I have regretted. I never told you that the morning after you left for New York, Harrison came here. He looked like he hadn't slept and the worry in his eyes was real. I sent him away, Nina. I was so angry for what he did that I didn't listen to him."

He came here? For me?

"What?"

"I didn't tell you because I wanted you to settle into your new life. You needed to leave, and if you knew that he came, that would have messed with you. I planned on telling you, but you seemed to have resolved that situation. You seemed happy. I didn't want to drudge up old hurt."

I pause before I respond. Hurt, anger, and confusion intermingle in an ugly knot in my stomach. I'm mostly surprised that Grammy would keep something like this from me. Maybe if I had known, I would have had the closure I've been seeking ever since that night. I sigh.

"What happened to me with Harrison shaped every relationship I've ever had with a man. I don't trust. I don't allow them in to get to know me. I'm petrified of getting hurt so deeply again, but most of all, if they know the real me, then they might leave me." Tears trickle down my face. Jesus, I thought after last night I was all dried up.

"Oh, baby girl! I thought I was doing the right thing. Sometimes when we try to protect the ones we love, we end up doing more damage. This is all my fault. Now I see that all it did was hurt you more. I am so sorry." She hugs me tightly. "Nina, Harrison knows the real you. He sees you." She backs away from me and holds my hands. "Now, I know I haven't been in a relationship in ages, but what I know is that when someone sees you, really sees you, then it's important for you to give them a chance to make the past right. Let him."

"He has tried, but I continually shut him down. I'm too scared. What am I going to do?"

"Oh, my sweet girl, I can't tell you what to do. Trust your heart. Stop letting those negative thoughts take up viable real estate in your head."

That is exactly what I'm afraid to do.

Nina

Fifteen Years Ago

I'm leaving. No hesitation in my actions. The big, fat envelope NYU sent was a sign. I received it a couple of months prior, and was going to share the news with Harrison. Early admittance. It's bittersweet. So much good is happening, and I have to make some choices. Harrison and I weren't an item. He didn't even follow through with the date. Sure, there's chemistry, but we didn't make anything official. I was excited and terrified to tell him about my early admittance to NYU. But now, after the scene at prom, I won't end up sharing anything with him. Obviously.

The idea of a change of scenery only solidifies my decision. The universe is really working in my favor. I don't want to leave Grammy, but she has always supported living my dreams.

Grammy helps me pack the same night, tears streaming down both of our faces. At one point, she holds my face in her hands, looks into my tear-filled eyes, and says, "Baby girl, you are making the right decision. As hard as it is to let you go, this will give you a new beginning in a place where you will find your tribe. Those people who will see your worth. Don't settle. What Harrison did was hurtful and despicable. He doesn't deserve any of your energy. Just make sure you guard that heart of yours, sweet girl. This is your first lesson in betrayal, and it won't be your last. I have no doubt you will make your own mark in the world and I'll be with you every step of the way."

I fall into Grammy's arms and sob. Crying because I'm leaving the only person who knows my heart. Crying because I allowed someone to see me after living in the shadows for years. Crying because I'm saying goodbye to the sweet, naïve girl who will never put herself in a place of vulnerability again.

Nina

Present Day

The dread permeating my body vibrates. I'm sweating. Addie would love the fact that I, in fact, am human and perspire. I chuckle at the notion. I take a last look at myself in the mirror. Satisfied that I don't look like I'm trying too hard, I exit my room, only to be accosted by the spicy scent of Harrison, who is chumming it up with Grammy again. These two have quite the relationship.

"Ready to go?" He greets me with an easy smile.

Butterflies. This is the effect he has on me. Every. Single. Time. No matter how I try to avoid it, it comes back to the flutters. I quickly regain my composure.

"Sure. Grammy, do you need anything while we're out?" I try to distract myself from my internal struggle to stay calm and cool.

"No, you all have fun. By the way, I'm going out tonight. There's speed-dating bingo at the senior center. I'm going with Mildred."

I tilt my head at her. "Is that even a thing?"

"It is, and I hope there is some fresh meat."

What?!

Harrison chuckles.

Before I can ask more questions—because let's be honest, I have many—Harrison grabs my hand to lead me out the front door while Grammy continues to grin at me like a lunatic. Is it too early for a cocktail?

Harrison

I continue to laugh as we get in my rental car, especially since Nina appears to be speechless, which rarely occurs. I decide to throw caution to the wind and break the ice.

"So, Grammy is in the market for some action," I deadpan.

Nina turns her head, eyes narrowed, and says, "Don't say a word. I can't wrap my head around her speed dating. What is happening? I mean she's probably going to get more action than me. Seriously, can't remember the last time I actually went on a date."

Realizing the amount of information she just vomited, she throws her hand up to her mouth to stop the running dialogue. I grin. Lots of good information to work with as we continue to ride out of town.

"A little dry spell? Interesting."

"I am *not* discussing my dating life with you. I'm just surprised that Grammy is getting out there. I mean, when I was growing up, she never went out on a date even years after Gramps died."

"Well, she is an attractive woman. It really shouldn't be a surprise that she's putting herself out there."

She exhales audibly. "I know. I'm happy for her. Honestly, I love that she's living such a vibrant life. I suppose it just confirms how much I've missed being in New York."

We ride the rest of the way in comfortable silence. It makes me wish we could move forward because I know we could have something real. Something genuine. I'm *never* comfortable with silence in the presence of women I'm attracted to, mostly because there's no substance to my interest. Nina's different. Nina's the whole package. But there is so much bullshit to wade through, and my biggest fear is that we can never simply be us. I shake those thoughts away as I pull into a parking spot at this hole-in-the-wall diner.

"This looks interesting."

"This is my go-to place when I want to be away from the prying eyes of our beloved town. The bonus is that they have the best, smothered, country-fried chicken I have ever had. That is something I can't find in the city." My stomach rumbles at the notion.

"I thought you said it was a new place and you just heard about it."

"I don't want anyone to know about this place, so I pretend it's a new discovery. I trust that you won't divulge my secret."

"You don't have to worry about that. But the food you're talking about … no wonder you and Addie are kindred spirits. Do they have salads? Grammy is killing me with her home cooking."

Is she serious?

"I bet they have some wilted iceberg and some tomato that will meet your ridiculous demands." I laugh.

"Whatever. I suppose another meal inviting a cardio episode into my life isn't going to kill me … yet. Of course, I can keep your secret. I'm a vault."

"That's the spirit, Nina. Throw caution to the wind." I wink.

Nina

Look, my Grammy dating was a lot of information, and along with eating like crap, my whole persona is completely out of whack. Harrison needs to cut me some slack. But no, he keeps pushing the fucking envelope. Typical. He's like a magnet. I can't avoid his pull, but we're too far gone to be anything but business associates and, maybe, friends. He's convincing me of that more and more.

I peruse the grease-laden menu. The diner appears clean, but the décor screams, "I love the '70s." No, really, it does. Dark paneling accentuates the restaurant with red-leather booths sprinkled throughout, complemented by random accessories from the period. There are disco balls dangling from the ceiling. I'm waiting for the Bee Gees to pop out and break out into some sort of montage of their greatest hits.

The waitress comes to take our order, and as I'm about to speak, the Neanderthal sitting across from me orders for me. What. The. Fuck. Not only does he order for me, but he orders that smothered, country-fried crap that he was going on and on about in the car. I had my heart set on the house salad. Okay, not really, because I'm sure their house salad is from a bag, but seriously, I can speak for myself.

She writes down the order and leaves us to ourselves just as I'm about to change mine to a salad.

"Before you say anything, I ordered for you because that salad is probably old and rotting, which you would hate, so you're welcome." He grins. I can't handle those dimples.

I sigh and shake my head. I might as well just sit in the passenger seat of my life since my power to make decisions has come to an end.

"I'm going to cut to the chase. Melanie and I are not together, nor will we ever be, so I just wanted to put that out there. My parents have some delusional ideas that they're trying to push on me."

Color me curious. I know I'm going to regret this, but I feel the nudge to inquire as to what the amazing Bitsy and Lyle McCall have cooking up for the H-man.

"Well, what on earth are they trying to do? Arrange a marriage? Does she have some goats or cows that will be accompanying her?" I chuckle, imagining Melanie hanging out with a load of farm animals. As I continue to laugh, I notice that Harrison's face is super serious. Obviously my joke fell flat.

"Well, aside from the livestock, you hit the nail on the head."

"What? Don't they know that arranged marriages aren't even a thing in this country? Plus, you are an established, successful businessman. You don't need them."

He looks at me with a flash of vulnerability, and then it quickly disappears.

"Look, I think they're pushing this because they're in financial trouble, and by me marrying the witch, they'll have a financial empire. My father literally used the word 'empire' when he explained his plans to me. Here's the catch. My father is holding something about you over my head. He threatened to expose you. He told me whatever it is would ruin you."

I tilt my head at him. He's serious. Me? Secrets? The only secret I have is that I still like boy bands, which I will not be sharing with him.

Wait … no. Shit. Shit. Shit. Lyle couldn't possibly know about what happened five years ago. Nobody knows except the parties involved.

I compose myself and say, "Seriously? Harrison, I don't have any secrets. I'm possibly the most boring human on the planet. Your father is blowing smoke up your ass. He's got nothing."

"I wouldn't describe you as boring, Nina. On the contrary, I think you're the most exciting and fascinating woman I've ever met."

I hear myself gasp at this admission, and the words just hang there. Harrison's gaze bores into mine. The moment is cut short as the waitress brings our meals with a side of cardiac arrest. Okay, I have to admit it smells divine—more divine than a house salad—and when I cut into it, the juices from the plump chicken seep out, and I might have moaned. Okay, I moaned. I hate when he's right.

"Don't tell Addie I'm eating this. She won't let me forget it," I say, my eyes closed as I enjoy the party that is currently happening in my mouth.

"Your secret is safe with me." I look at him and he winks at me. I need to get out of here.

"Well, I'm sorry that your family resembles an episode of *Dynasty*, but I can tell you that they don't know any secrets about me, so you're free and clear." What a lie. I smirk at him.

"I did ask Jameson to get his PI friend, Grady, involved just to cover all my bases."

"You did what! You have no right to look into things about me, Harrison. You and I, we're nothing. We're barely friends, so whatever your fucked-up family is cooking up, you can leave me out of it." My stomach launches into acidic anxiety mode, and the food on the table suddenly looks awful. I can't stay here another minute. "I've lost my appetite. I need to get back to Grammy's and get some work done." I *knew* I couldn't trust this man.

I get up from the table as Harrison throws some money on the table. Silence blankets the car as we drive back. I stare out the window in total disbelief. The thought that maybe we could become something evaporates as I'm reminded that his family will always have power over him, no matter who else they destroy. Now I need to figure out how to keep the biggest mistake of my life under lock and key.

Nina

I barely wait for the car to stop before I yank open the door. I don't say goodbye. I don't thank him for lunch. I just escape, ignoring his stuttering behind me. It feels good to slam the door on his voice.

I run to the front door, throw it open, and scream my frustration into the house. I'm attacked by hugs and kisses from … not Grammy. When my eyes regain focus, I'm greeted with three faces: Addie, Owen, and George. *Oh my God!*

"Jesus, you all scared the shit out of me. What the hell are you doing here?"

"Nina, we missed you!" Addie says, smiling widely. "And besides, I can write anywhere, so we thought we would pop in and see the town that grew you."

"Where's your appendage?" I grin at her as I hug Owen. He seriously should get an award for being the world's best hugger.

"What? You don't think Jameson and I can be away from each other? Okay. He had to travel to Boston with a client. He's going to join us at the end of the week."

"Owen, stop hogging her. Come here, Nina, and give George a big hug." George looks like an Armani ad.

He squeezes me tightly, and when he releases me, he narrows his eyes. I can't let him look too long; he'll see I have a problem right away.

Addie takes her turn in the hugging department. She sniffs me and pulls back.

"You ate something fried."

"Jesus, what are you, the food FBI? Yes, I had country-fried chicken for lunch with Harrison."

"We'll come back to the food issue. Let's talk about the tidbit that you were with Big H." She wiggles her eyebrows.

"Don't call him that. We were having lunch to clear the air. There's a lot of drama with his family and he was getting me up to speed. Apparently, his family has dirt on me and is using it to blackmail Harrison into marrying Melanie, the one his parents forced him to dump me for on prom night."

Everyone openly stares at me.

"I feel like I just walked into the middle of one of the *Real Housewives* shows," George says. "You know, I just love it when those bitches start throwing shit."

Leave it to George to add humor to a bizarre situation.

"I'm bored. Addie, you told me we would have fun, and all you're doing is talking. Where is the fun?"

"Yeah, Addie, where is the fun? You realize that you brought him to the armpit of the country." I laugh at her.

"Please, surely there's something fun to do here. Cow tipping? Hanging out in the parking lot watching traffic go by? What did you do growing up?"

"I read and hung out at the library."

"I thought I was the lame one in this relationship. Your grammy sounds fun, I bet she'll have some ideas. Where is she? I can't wait to meet her and get all the dirt on you."

"She's at speed-dating bingo."

George's and Addie's eyes widen. Their mouths form an O.

"That's a thing? *Oh my God!*"

"Are there hot chicks there? I like bingo," Owen says with mischief in his eyes.

I shake my head. "Owen, this is at the senior citizens' center. All the ladies are too old for you."

"Says you. Age doesn't matter when you are in love."

I can't really argue with that. But all my New York friends being here only adds a layer of anxiety to my problems.

Harrison

After Nina slams the car door in my face, I go for a drive. Maybe she's right. We have been dancing around each other for over a decade, and it just seems that we'll never be together. She has walls. I have walls. Neither of us trust fully, and frankly, she deserves somebody who doesn't have all this baggage, someone who doesn't continually hurt her. Was it my imagination or did she pale when I told her that my father has information that could ruin her?

I'm jolted back to reality by the incessant ringing of my phone. Without looking at who it is, I answer, "Harrison here."

"Somebody sounds like they have sunshine radiating out of their ass," Jameson says.

"You've been with Addie too long. You're starting to talk like her."

"Speaking of my beautiful fiancée, have you seen her yet?"

"Why would I see her?"

"She, George, and Owen are in your quaint town as we speak. Addie figured a change of scenery would help her write, so she dragged Owen and George with her."

"I bet Nina's going to love that."

"So what has crawled up your ass besides your dysfunctional family trying to force you into marriage?"

"Well, I think that would be enough, but I've also come to the realization that Nina and I are on two different planes … maybe in two different worlds. As much as I want to be with her, our timing is never right."

"Look, I've known for a while that there was something between you and Nina, so if you want it to work, you have to make an effort. All I hear are excuses."

"As much as that makes sense, I think the best thing for me to do is to clean up my family mess and move on. Maybe find a girlfriend. A real one." The words don't feel right coming out of my mouth.

"Glad I'm sitting down, because in all the years knowing you, that is the first time I've ever heard the word 'girlfriend' from you."

"Maybe you and Addie inspire me," I lie.

"Whatever you need to tell yourself. The reason for my call is to tell you Grady will be in touch with you by the end of the week with an update."

"Great. Thanks, Jameson."

"Take good care of my girl, and Owen will probably want you to assume the role as his wingman. Oh, and I'll be there at the end of the week, too. I thought we could all fly to Vegas together."

I laugh. "Happy to be his wingman. Maybe it can be mutually beneficial. I'm looking forward to Vegas. I need a little distraction from my reality."

We end the call. If I'm ready to move on, why do I feel so empty?

Nina

While Owen is trying to convince us to head over to the senior citizens' center, Grammy walks in and settles her eyes on the group sitting in her living room. Before I can make any introductions, Addie springs from the couch like an eager kangaroo and accosts my grandmother. Okay. She doesn't accost her, but she does hug her fiercely as if they've already met a hundred times before.

"You must be Addie! Oh, you're exactly how Nina described you." Grammy beams at her.

"Did she describe me as a woman who needs constant assistance dressing and tries to bring her over to the dark side of eating fried foods instead of that kale crap?"

"Oh, Addie, I love you already! You know, she has been eating lots of my home cooking, and it's fried heaven!"

"Grammy, I love you! Together we will help her see the light." Addie's eyes are dancing, and the two of them together might scare me a little bit.

Grammy steps out of the embrace and turns her eyes to Owen and George. Both are grinning at her, waiting their turn. She greets them as enthusiastically as she did Addie, as if they're all old friends. The house is brimming with love.

"Alright, I hope you all are hungry. I'm making fried chicken, mashed potatoes, and green beans, along with some homemade buttermilk biscuits."

"You had me at fried." Addie's cheeks are pink with excitement. I roll my eyes because she might never leave now that Grammy has gotten her claws into her.

"Owen, can you help me?"

He grins at her and rushes to her side. "Yes. Can you take me to the senior citizens' center with you? I like bingo and hot girls."

She giggles at him. "Well, maybe after you all get back from Vegas, but right now, we need to fix dinner. Nina, Lillie and Maddie are set to arrive in about an hour."

Why is it that I am the last to know about EVERYTHING? Apparently, I'm merely in the supporting cast for the play about my life.

"They're going to check into the B&B before coming over. I invited Harrison for dinner, as well." Her eyes sparkle.

Of course she did.

My phone pings and I finally feel a small amount of relief.

Nina

I haven't heard from Captain Morgan in a few days. Not since our introduction. To be completely transparent, I was a little disappointed, but he had shared that he works a lot, and I truly understand how difficult that can make things. Still, with all the trust issues that blanket me, I feel ghosted. I excuse myself to go upstairs to freshen up, giddy with anticipation of his message.

I settle on my bed and open the app's message center to read his message.

> *Captain Morgan: I am so sorry for my lapse in connecting. Honestly, my life has gotten a tad more complicated as I travel. Would you be available to chat tonight? Say around ten? I know it's late, and I will totally understand if that doesn't work for you.*

It's like we're cut from the same cloth. I'm excited about how attracted I am to his honesty.

Me: *I understand how work and travel can make things more difficult, so no apology necessary. I would be happy to meet you in the chat room at ten tonight. I look forward to it.*

I close the app and head downstairs. Maybe this is exactly the distraction I need from Harrison. Moving on and moving forward. As I revel in my new epiphany, I hear the arrival of Lillie and Maddie and head downstairs.

Maddie is already engaged with Owen. While on the autism spectrum, she is bright and funny even though she's nonverbal. She communicates by sign language, which I was happy to learn. She is petite, for a six year old, but she is determined and fierce with her wide blue eyes, her ready smile, and her Shirley Temple blond curls. She's happy, and that has everything to do with Lillie. Owen knows sign language, as well, since he was nonverbal until he was five. He's kept it up all his life. Addie and Lillie have formed an instant connection. I love this group of people.

Maddie sees me and bounces over to hug me. While normally reserved with touch, she's affectionate with those she knows best. There is so much love in this room that I can't help but feel unworthy of it all. Lillie grabs my hand and squeezes it.

"Did you ladies have a good trip?" I sign as I speak to them.

"It was great. Maddie loved flying first class and meeting the crew. Thank you for doing that for us."

I watch Maddie go back over to Owen, where he launches into his story about flying to Boston first class last year and showing her his Instagram account, where he has over a million followers. He is something else.

"Ready for Vegas?" Her eyes sparkle with mischievous.

"No, but I will be, and I suppose you've been talking to Addie. Seriously, you all need to stop talking about me."

She laughs at me. I need to reevaluate this boss-assistant relationship.

"Grammy has graciously offered to watch Maddie while I work from here. This is a great change of scenery for us and ideal since school is out for the week."

"I'm just sorry that we're leaving while you're here."

"It's only for the weekend, and then when you come back, you need to tell me all the dirt." She wiggles her eyebrows at me.

"Nothing is going to happen. Besides, I've started chatting with someone on that dating site. In fact, I have a chat set up for tonight."

"Oh, well, I can't wait to hear all about it."

"Can't wait to hear all about what?" Harrison's voice surprises me. When did he get here?

I sigh.

"Nothing you need to know. Just business."

At that moment, my cousin Mason and his mother, my Aunt Tabby enter the room and I rush to greet them. I had no idea that they were coming as well, but Grammy is always up for keeping me on my toes. My aunt smells like lemons and love. I know that love doesn't have a real scent, but I think it's whatever makes one smile. She is such an amazing human, and I can't wait for Lillie to connect with her. I turn to Mason, who isn't big on hugs but graciously accommodates my need to embrace him.

I notice that he isn't looking at me, he's looking at Lillie and the staring is mutual. Ah, maybe I can play matchmaker. We all gather at the table with an abundance of food. I'm overwhelmed by these people and the intensity of gratitude I feel at this very moment. I might be a tad nervous about the whole Vegas experience, but tonight I can simply be in the moment.

Nina

Everyone heads back to the B&B with their stomachs full and their hearts even fuller. It was a magical night. The house was full of conversation and love. It was the first time in a very long while that I felt at home again.

"Grammy, thank you for dinner. It was so wonderful getting to be with everyone."

"You've surrounded yourself with good people, and I am so proud of you."

"Thank you. I'm so lucky to have found this eclectic group of people. Also, I appreciate you for being willing to watch Maddie while Lillie works. I know that is so helpful since she's a single mom."

"I'm happy to do it. She is such a magical child, just like Owen. What I wouldn't give to have the beautiful outlook they both do. Did you notice Mason staring at Lillie?"

"I did! The staring was very much reciprocated."

"Mason deserves someone kind. Anyway, I am headed off to bed. Speeding-dating bingo was exhausting, but well worth it." Her eyes twinkle.

"Sounds like a successful day for you." I am secretly hoping she isn't going to elaborate.

"Oh, it was successful. I have a date tomorrow morning." She giggles like a schoolgirl.

"Date? You seniors move quick. Where are you going? What's his name? I need to put a location tracker on your phone."

She glares at me. "Girly, I am going out to breakfast with a nice gentlemen named Marvin, and you will not be putting a location tracker on my phone. He is widowed, with no children. He still drives, which is a huge bonus, and he is sex on a stick." She wiggles her eyebrows. What is happening here?

I could have gone my whole life not hearing my grandmother utter "sex on a stick."

"On that disturbing note, I'm going upstairs to get ready for bed. I hope you enjoy Marvin. I mean, have a good breakfast. Don't go enjoying him until you know him better. Oh my God, I need to stop talking."

I run up the stairs to escape as her laughter follows me.

It's 9:45, and I'm nervous. I have brushed my teeth, washed my face, gotten into my pajamas, and am waiting for the minutes to slowly tick by until I can log on to the app.

Inhale the good shit. Exhale the bullshit. In and out, I breathe like I'm the Dalai Lama. I'm hoping it will help me relax. My phone pings, indicating that he's on, and I eagerly open the chat.

> Captain Morgan: I'm so glad we could finally "meet."
> Me: I am too. Where shall we start? I know, let's play twenty questions.
> Captain Morgan: Okay. I'll start. What's your favorite color?
> Me: Red. It's a powerful color and makes a statement. You?
> Captain Morgan: Blue. Mostly because it goes with gray and black suits well, but it also represents depth, trust, loyalty, and stability.

What? Holy shit. Color talk is getting deep.

Me: *Wow, Captain, you are getting profound with your color choice, but I will say that I love those attributes. And obviously you agree that a color can be so powerful yet so beautiful.*

Captain Morgan: Colors say a lot about a person. They make a nonverbal statement.

Me: *You can't seriously judge a person by their color selection, can you?*

Captain Morgan: No, but it can be indicative of who they are. I use it in business all the time, and it's served me well.

Me: *Well, you have given me a lot to think about, and now I'm scared about my color selections. LOL!*

Captain Morgan: I think your choice says good things about you. Red is such a romantic color, as well as powerful.

Is it possible to swoon over a chat? I know this is a superficial chat, but it feels effortless. I feel relaxed.

We chat for over two hours. Sometimes it's pretty deep, but most of the exchange is light, fun, and easy. It's refreshing. We set up a time for tomorrow night and I close the app with a smile on my face.

I fall into a content sleep with a smile on my face and the thought of Captain Morgan running through my head.

Nina

The week sped by with work—it never truly stops, does it? —and spending time with my tribe. We ate, played games, and I showed them my hometown. Granted, the tour wasn't much, but George was enthralled with Marley and Cassie's boutique. He even bought a few pieces to take back to New York, along with the promise of buying more. I even managed to avoid Harrison for the most part. He was present for some of our dinners but was too busy grilling Grammy's new friend, Marvin. Yes, they apparently are an item. It is taking me a while to wrap my head around that one.

Friday morning, I wake up with pep in my step and a smile on my face—until I remember where I'm headed today. Vegas. The site where mistakes happen and are left to fester. In my case, my mishap is never to be talked about again. I'm just hoping I don't happen to run into that particular bump in the road.

No more thoughts about the mistake that shall not be mentioned … ever. This trip is about celebrating Addie and Jameson. This is going to be fun, and I seriously need some fun. Am I convincing enough?

I head downstairs with my bags, including the one left in Harrison's trunk. It mysteriously appeared and I have a sneaking suspicion that he intentionally held it hostage. I was too stubborn to ask him about it. I simply ignored the fact that my selection of handbags and various accessories were missing. I enter the kitchen where I'm immediately greeted by Grammy, Lillie, and Maddie, the three chatting it up like old friends. Lillie has been teaching my grandmother sign language and Maddie is enjoying helping with that process.

"Good morning!" They all turn to greet me while Lillie presents me with a mug of steaming-hot coffee.

"Morning! Ready for the big trip?" Lillie grins at me.

"I suppose. Anything I need to know before I go?" Work mode always relaxes me.

"No, we're good. You have some new clients I've set up video chats with for next week, but you're free this weekend. Go relax and have fun! You deserve it."

"Well, you can call me if anything comes up."

"Nina, I'm not going to call you unless someone's dying. So, how was your chat last night?"

Fortunately, Grammy is distracted by Maddie. I certainly don't need an inquisition before I leave.

"It was good." I try to be cool, but the smile that spreads across my face has a mind of its own. "We talked for two hours. In fact, that has been our timetable all week."

"Oh, Nina. That's wonderful. I'm so happy for you!"

"We have a chat date on Monday. I like him, Lillie."

She grabs my hand and squeezes it. "You deserve nothing but happiness. Just remember, in order to receive it, you must be open to it. It's scary but worth it."

"Lillie, you are one very wise woman."

"Experience, my friend. Lots and lots of experience."

Grammy interrupts our conversation to let me know we need to get going. I finish off my coffee and we head out the door. I send up a little prayer that this trip will not be my undoing.

Harrison

We're all settled into the chartered plane but still waiting on Nina. Addie got a text saying she's almost here. I don't know why I feel so nervous. Nina has made it abundantly clear that we can't be together, but for some reason I don't feel deterred. And that alone freaks me out a little.

My thoughts stall as she enters the plane. She looks gorgeous with her off-the-shoulder sweater exposing her alabaster skin and those tight skinny jeans that don't leave much to the imagination. Her face bare of makeup and her hair gathered in a high ponytail, she is stunning. Wait. She's grinning. Nina doesn't grin.

Addie leaps from her seat and hugs Nina as if they hadn't seen each other just last night.

"Damn, girl, you look hot!" George bellows, then kisses her on the cheek.

Nina smiles at him. "Thanks, George. Sorry I'm late, guys. I was going over some work items with Lillie and lost track of the time."

She settles into the seat next to me. I purposely arranged it that way. What? You would too if you were me. It's the only way I'm going to have a chance at getting close to her, regardless of her constant rebuffs. I inhale her sweet, floral scent.

"You're awfully smiley this morning. Excited about our trip to Vegas?" I smirk at her.

"Of course I am. Super excited!" She grins at me.

She is throwing me off my game. Something has happened in the twelve hours since I've seen her. She's smiling and she doesn't seem annoyed by me. Could this mean I'm somehow losing ground with her? The idea terrifies me.

Harrison

I spent the last few hours observing the woman who is currently sleeping on my shoulder, with drool at the corner of her mouth. A mouth I would very much like to devour. Baby steps. She's a definite flight risk. We touch down, and I gently go to wake her, which isn't necessary as Addie screams, "We're here, bitches! Vegas here we come!"

Nina awakens with a jolt and meets my eyes. We have a nanosecond where we linger, and I wish it would last. Then reality jolts us and we gather our belongings to head toward the cars that will take us to the hotel. I booked two penthouse suites at the Bellagio for George, Nina, Owen, and myself. I put the happy couple in the Fountain View room where they will enjoy prime viewing of the famous Bellagio fountains and the Strip. Since the Penthouse Suite has one bedroom, I reserved a Tower Deluxe Suite that connects to Nina's penthouse, adding an additional bedroom for George and Owen. I'll be next door, which gives me the ability to keep an eye on her. No, I'm not a creeper. It's just that Vegas can be a bit dangerous and I want her safe. Stop judging me.

I head to the front desk to check in while Owen is bouncing off the walls. He just saw some showgirls and he's begging Nina to take him to some of the shows. I smile at how she's hugging on him. Happiness looks good on her. Someday, I'm going to deserve that smile.

The bellhop takes our bags, and we cram into the elevator. Addie is climbing Jameson like a jungle gym—he was waiting for us in the lobby, and she hasn't stopped touching him since they reunited—Owen is grinning ear to ear, and George is telling Nina what she should wear tonight and how he'll fix her hair. Addie and Jameson get off first, as their suite is a floor below us. They don't even say goodbye, but I do remind them that dinner is at seven. I insert the card to get us to the Penthouse level. The elevator dings and opens to the most elegant space. Owen races in and immediately dives onto the couch. Nina gasps and points at me.

Harrison

The penthouse is stunning. A spacious marble foyer leads to the grand living area and separate dining room. Pops of color dot the room with artwork and accessories. Walls of windows cater to the Vegas skyline. It's breathtaking.

"So are we all staying here?" She tilts her head and bites her lower lip. So. Freaking. Sexy.

"Owen and George are in the connecting bedroom and I'm right next door. I figured it would be easiest. I hope you don't mind." I'm waiting for the usual Nina argument.

"I don't mind at all. It's amazing, Harrison. Thank you for arranging everything. I think I'll go freshen up."

What just happened? No argument. No sass. Just compliance. I don't like this at all.

"Well, seems your girl is a little giddy today," George says. "I wonder why … Maybe she met someone. You'd better up your game. She's not one to wait around for you to get your shit together."

"What makes you think that I want her?" I ask, trying to keep my voice even and my face expressionless.

"Oh, please! You are so transparent." He rolls his eyes and struts to his room.

This may be an extremely long weekend.

Nina

I'm in a festive mood even though I have a bit of apprehension that I may come face-to-face with one of my biggest mistakes. I know, I know. You're desperate to hear my secret, but it wouldn't be right to tell you and not my close friends, right? Thanks for understanding.

"Guurl! Where are you right now? Because you certainly aren't paying attention to all the glam I'm sprinkling you with, nor are you drinking." George looks at me with his hands on his hips and an eyebrow raised.

"Why aren't you bothering Addie? She's the one who needs help dressing."

We laugh together over that bit of truth.

"I'm not going near them. They're practically one unit. Besides, I already arranged her outfits in her suitcase like I would for a small child; plus, I have hair and makeup scheduled for her. She's all set, so I'm all yours."

"You know you don't have to do all this on your time off, George, although it's really nice to be taken care of like this."

"Honey, if I'm not styling, I'm thinking about it anyway! Let me do my thing."

I take a sip of champagne and peek at myself in the mirror. Woah! I'm hot. I know that sounds conceited, but George is like a magician. My hair is gathered at the nape of my neck in a tight bun. The red dress shimmers and is fitted in all the right areas with my back on display.

I grin at George and he beams at me. "Let's go, baby girl! We have some partying to do!"

We take a step out of my room and Owen grabs my hand. "Wow, I don't need a wingman, Harrison, because Nina is my date and she's hot."

I laugh. "Owen, what did Addie say about describing girls as hot? A lady likes to be complimented on how she looks. Saying things like, 'You look pretty' is so much better to hear."

"Addie, isn't here and you really look hot." He wiggles his eyebrows and I shake my head.

When I look up, Harrison is staring at me. "You look stunning!"

I'm surprised to hear something so open from him. No jabs, no jokes? "Thank you," I whisper. He looks delectable. His charcoal suit hugs his muscular frame, and his blue tie brings out his eyes. Blue tie. Loyalty. Trust. I shake my head to clear my thoughts. Tonight isn't about my complicated feelings regarding Harrison or my new infatuation with a certain Captain Morgan. No, tonight is about Addie and Jameson. I just need to keep reminding myself of that.

Harrison

We head down to The Mayfair Supper Club, a restaurant in the hotel. The ambience of the space is a tribute to the glamorous eras of Las Vegas and old New York. Its eclectic vibe is sexy and elegant. Addie and Jameson are already at the table with their lips locked. I clear my throat.

"Do you think that for a couple of hours, you could untangle yourselves from one another?" I chuckle as I say it. "You *are* staying in the same room, anyway. This isn't high school, lovers."

"Okay. But only because you asked nicely. Nina, holy shit, you look *hot*! Like sizzling. Like we may have to get bodyguards for you. Jesus, George you are a magician." Addie is practically screaming.

Nina's face lights up. "So, you like it? I wasn't sure if it was too much, but George said that this dress screamed Vegas."

Addie laughs. "That dress screams a lot of things. You're going to be a hit at the club later."

"What club are we going to?" Nina inquires. There was hesitation in her voice. Or maybe it was my imagination.

"Oh, it's a new club. Jameson knows the general manager and he got us a VIP booth. What's the name again?" She turns to her fiancé.

"It's called Allure. They just opened last week."

Nina's face goes pale and all the light that was shining so bright from her has quickly dimmed. My thoughts are interrupted by Owen, who bellows about how he's starving. What are you hiding, Nina, and why does it scare you so much?

*A*llure. It can't be the same. It must be a coincidence. *Okay, Nina, this night is about your two dearest friends. There's nothing to worry about, so let's have some fun!* My internal dialogue is having a battle of wills.

I demand my thoughts be in the present moment, so I observe the intimate, romantic décor around me. I sip my martini while I peruse the menu. More like stare blankly at the words. Hunger has escaped me. Everyone is engaged in conversation except Harrison, who is staring at me with concern creasing his brow. I can say all I want about how we can't be together, but this man knows when I'm off my game. He knows when I'm faking.

I smile at him and say, "You've done an outstanding job of arranging everything. The penthouse is breathtaking and I love the vibe of this restaurant."

"Well, it's the least I can do. Are you excited about going to the new club?"

"A club is a club. How different can it be? In fact, I may go for a bit but head back to the penthouse. I'm exhausted," I lie.

"Well, I heard this club stands out from the others. Don't be a party pooper. Hang out with us. You know Owen is going to want a dance partner." He grins.

"Owen will have no problem finding someone to dance with him."

"Nina, we're going to have fun. I promise."

"Hurry up, guys! I need to dance and find some hot girls!" Owen is vibrating with excitement.

"You heard the man! Let's order dinner and then head out to the club," Harrison says as he fist-bumps Owen.

Nina

I have been to a lot of clubs, but Allure is different. It's sultry. It's sexy. From the white-leather booths to the multi-tier dance floor, it's like a sex den on steroids. And now I'm sure what I was afraid of is true.

Owen's eyes are bulging at this very moment at the scantily clad waitresses. I want to throw my hands over his eyes, but he's always reminding us that he's a man. And so he is. We'll all be on high alert to make sure no one takes advantage of him. He's precious and trusting.

We skip the line and are escorted to our own VIP area. I'm thrilled not to have to be shoulder to shoulder with a crowd of people. Sweaty, gross people. Before I get comfortable, Harrison presents me with a martini, perfectly prepared with my signature two olives. Before I can thank him, I'm met with a pair of familiar dark eyes. Oh shit. I can't believe this happened so quickly. I had a sinking feeling this was his club. After all, we talked about it the entire weekend we were together. Are you confused? You won't be in a minute.

"Nina, I heard you were in town and hoped you would grace me with your presence. You look stunning." He takes my hand and kisses it. His eyes never leave mine. I gasp. I hear a throat clear behind me and realize our whole group is staring at the two of us.

"Pardon my manners. I am Antonio Rossi, and this is my club. Welcome! Please, anything you want tonight is my gift to you."

Can I pause this scene for a small moment? Antonio is sex on a stick. Seriously. His dark wavy hair begs to be touched. His tall, muscular frame is accentuated with charcoal pants and a crisp, white shirt unbuttoned low enough to catch a glimpse of his amazing chest. Yes, friends, before you ask, we had a small thing. That's all I'm saying about it because it was one of the biggest mistakes of my life.

"Are you Nina's boyfriend? I'm going to have to fight you because she was mine first." Leave it to Owen to break the uncomfortable silence. I grin at him with gratefulness.

"No, Owen, Antonio is most certainly not my boyfriend. I met him the last time I was here, and it's simply a surprise to see him. Anyway, thanks so much for coming over and we appreciate your hospitality."

Antonio releases my hand and I exhale.

"Nina, I would like a dance tonight. I have some things to take care of, but I'll be back for you. We need to catch up."

I don't look at him but simply nod. Yes, I'm sure a conversation is in order, but I would have loved for my group to have not been exposed to this exchange.

As he walks away, I cautiously make eye contact with my tablemates, take a gulp of my martini, and get ready for the inquisition.

Harrison

Well, that exchange was certainly interesting. Seriously, who the hell was that guy? I wanted to rip his hand off when he touched Nina, and the way he devoured her with his eyes—well, that made me crazy. I watched her face pale as he approached, but it didn't seem like she was afraid of him, more like she wanted to avoid him. He's in love with her. I could see it in his eyes. It's the same look Jameson gives Addie. My heart cracks a bit.

The moment he walks away, the table erupts with questions shooting off like bullets. Nina holds up her hands as a way of silencing the chaos.

"I am sure you all have things you'd like to ask, but right now, I really don't want to talk about it."

"Well, Nina, you don't get that luxury. First of all, Mr. Hottie comes over here all sultry and sexy—"

"Addie …" Jameson interrupts.

"Honey, you're sultry and sexy, too. I'm simply trying to get my point across. Anyway, he comes over as if he owns you or wants to own you. I practically had an orgasm watching the interaction. Spill."

Jameson shakes his head. George laughs and Owen begs to get on the dance floor. I'm stone silent.

"I think Owen and I are going to hit the dance floor, but that doesn't mean I don't get to know the scoop." George eyes Nina.

"Don't worry, George, I'll get the story," Addie says, her eyes intense. She can be scary when she wants to be.

"Okay, kids. Play nice." He and Owen descend the stairs to the dance floor.

"Nina, how do you know him?" Addie asks.

"I met him when I was here about a year ago for that literary agent conference. It was no big deal. We met, had a few dates, hooked up, and then I left," Nina says matter-of-factly.

"That sounds boring, and that man doesn't exude mundane. He exudes hot, sweaty sex. Jameson, I am suddenly exhausted. Do you mind if we call it a night?" Then she winks. "This conversation is not over, Nina," Addie says more sternly as she points at her.

"I was under no delusional that we were done. Get some 'rest'." Nina uses air quotes on the word *rest*.

And then it's just the two of us. Her body tenses. She turns toward me, looks me in the eye, and says, "I suppose you want to interrogate me now."

I surprise myself by saying, "It's your story to tell, and when you're ready, I hope you know that you can tell me."

Nina

I'm surprised and touched by Harrison's response. If the roles were reversed, I don't know that I could be so calm.

"I think I'll head back to my room. I'm feeling worn out."

"Not like Addie, right?" He laughs.

"Oh my God! She was ridiculous. I thought she was going to combust." I giggle.

We head over to the dance floor to let George and Owen know that we're leaving. They're surrounded by women and Owen is in heaven. George assures us he will supervise the dancing man, aka Owen, and that they won't be staying much longer. Good luck, George. Owen appears to be a hot commodity.

We walk out of the club and hope not to be accosted by Antonio. I'm just not up to his, well, everything. He's intense and smoldering. But oddly, I don't feel anything like I do in Harrison's presence. Sigh. I'm a mess.

Safely in the elevator, we remain silent. I'm grateful for the reprieve. We step off the elevator and into the penthouse where Harrison turns to me and whispers, "Good night. I hope you sleep well." He walks to his bedroom, and while I want to be alone, there is a loss I feel as he leaves the room.

I close the door to my room and shed my evening attire in exchange for my comfy pajamas. In the bathroom, I gaze at my reflection and wonder how I'm going to explain the mess my life seems to be. Cool, confident Nina has really fucked up. Will Harrison hate me? Why am I even worried about what he thinks? We aren't anything. At least, that's what I keep telling myself, but then I have these reactions to him, like feeling alone when he leaves the room. I wonder what Captain Morgan would say about my situation. Would he judge me?

Heading back into the bedroom, I grab my phone and throw myself on the bed. Sleep will be futile, and I must talk to someone impartial. Someone who doesn't know me well. The reality is that tomorrow, I'll need to sit down with Antonio because, well, he is persistent and intense. I've got to head him off. And anyway, he won't leave me alone until he has his opportunity to meet with me.

I settle on the bed as I log in to the dating app hoping Captain Morgan is available. Maybe he can provide some male insight. I tap on his name and type.

Me: Are you available to talk? Need a friend.

I stare at the screen as if it's a magic ball and will provide me the answers I need. Time ticks away and I realize that maybe it's a sign he's not available. Then I hear a ping and look down.

Captain Morgan: I'm happy to hear from you. It's been an odd night, so I could use a distraction.
Me: Well, maybe we're both in need of a friend. I'm sorry to bother you. Really. We can just talk on Monday.
Captain Morgan: Wait. You said you needed a friend, so here I am.

Me: *Have you ever done anything you're so ashamed of that you cover it up and don't even tell your family and friends?*

Captain Morgan: *Woah. We go from our favorite colors to this. We aren't talking murder, are we? I can't be an accomplice to that. I'm joking. Maybe. Lay it on me.*

I laugh and relax a little. He's so easy to talk to.

Me: *Well, I'm on a trip with my group of best friends and we ran into someone from my past. Someone I had a brief relationship with, and we made a huge error in judgement. Well, I did. He seems to think otherwise. Anyway, this happened over a year ago and I thought he moved past it, but he hasn't. I saw him tonight and he wants to meet. My friends are all confused since I kept this a secret. What am I going to do?*

I see the dots bouncing to indicate he's typing, and then they stop. They start and stop again. I can hardly take the anticipation of what he's going to say. This was a mistake. I was reactive. I should have never contacted him. He probably thinks I'm a lunatic. I *am* a lunatic. A crazy, certifiable woman who is destined to be alone. And why, why would I ever tell him about this thing with another man? Lunatic. I hear a ping.

Captain Morgan: *Wow, Olive. You don't hold back. That certainly is a lot to process, but as your friend, I think having a conversation with him is key before anything else. Sometimes life has a funny way of showing up. It's surprising and confusing.*

Me: *You are very wise, Captain. What about my friends?*

Captain Morgan: *Be honest. Trust them to be there for you.*

Me: *Thank you. I feel like I can trust you and that isn't easy for me.*

Captain Morgan: I'm glad you feel that way, but it's probably because we're hidden by a screen. I hope you continue to feel that way even after we meet.

Me: You want to meet me? Even after I just vomited the mess of my existence on this chat?

Captain Morgan: Life is meant to be messy. Maybe I can help you clean it up? Look, you can do this. Be brave. Goodnight, Olive.

Me: Goodnight, Captain Morgan.

My heart is beating so fast. He said all the right things. He knew what I needed to hear, even though it was difficult to listen to. Tomorrow will come soon enough. I just hope that I'm as brave as Captain Morgan thinks I am.

Harrison

I'm pacing like a caged animal. Ever since the scene at the club where Antonio caressed Nina's hand and insinuated a past with her, I've been internally seething. Is this the big secret that my father alluded to? No. It can't be. She seemed like she didn't want him. Did he hurt her? If he touched her, I will kill him. *Breathe.* I need to relax.

I was the epitome of a supportive friend tonight. I did not react. Trying to be there for her without pushing for more information sucked the life out of me. My phone pings. It's the app Lillie told me about when I dropped by Nina's office a few weeks ago. I caught her while she was in the middle of a chat with her online boyfriend. She begged me not to tell Nina what she was doing, and in the process, told me about how it works. *What the hell*, I thought, *I'll give it a shot.* The conversation I had with my "match" was light and fun. She seems interesting and driven like I am. The whole time we were "chatting," Nina wasn't in my thoughts. That says something. This woman is intriguing.

I didn't realize I was still logged into the app, but I'm grateful for the distraction.

Olive is asking for a friend. Anything to help me not think of Nina. As the conversation progresses, I can't help but linger on the edge of confusion. Deja vu, anyone?

What. Is. Happening? Olive … Nina? This seems too coincidental. Jesus. No. This isn't Nina. Maybe Olive just had a similar situation. Sounds legit, right? I know. It doesn't at all. I sit and think about what I'm going to say. She needs a friend, so I suppose this is how I'll show up. Dishonest? Yes, but I can't tell her who I am now. Her night has been crazy enough.

I really want to say, "We love you, Nina, and we will always support you", but I keep quiet.

Ugh … this whole exchange makes me feel the opposite of trustworthy. And why did I just mention meeting her? I'll lose her for sure if she knows I'm carrying on this charade behind the screen.

As we say our goodnights, I'm suddenly saddened that she couldn't unburden herself with any of us.

Nina

Light seeps into my room in the morning. I stretch and am amazed at how well rested I feel. A smile tugs at my lips as I recall the chat exchange with Captain Morgan. He was exactly what I needed, and after all of my drama, he still wants to meet me. I gasp as I realize Addie and George are staring at me. Awesome.

"Spill, Bryant," Addie says. She is trying to look all serious, but I know she's bouncing with anticipation on the inside.

"Good morning to you both. Did you bring me coffee or is this the type of interrogation where you use unnecessary torture to make me talk?" I smirk.

George presents me with a piping-hot cup of coffee while Addie glares at him.

"What? I can't play good cop/bad cop, Addie. Look at her." George waves his hands up and down in front of me.

I must look like shit.

"Can I at least change my clothes and pee or is that not allowed?" I tilt my head at my adorable, quirky friend.

"Ugh. Go. Hurry up! I have been dying to know the story about the hot Italian stud since he came over to our table, and especially why that information was withheld from your best friends."

George cackles. "Baby girl, you used that man as your own inspiration for a night with *your* man, so don't *even* act like Nina's sideshow caused you to lose 'sleep' over it."

I giggle.

"I didn't hear Jameson complaining, and anyway, this isn't about me. This is about Nina hiding something important, and I think there's more to the story. So we're going to liquor her up, and she'll spill all the juicy details." They laugh and I sigh as I move toward the bathroom. "Oh, and put on your suit, since we're hanging by the pool today. Jameson got us a cabana with our own boy toy." Addie grins and wiggles her eyebrows.

I hope they have enough tequila at this hotel, because it sounds like it's going to be an extremely long day.

Nina

We head down to the pool, where we're greeted by Jameson and Harrison.

"Ladies, George, hope you all slept well?" Harrison eyes me. Not with his usual hardness but with a soft gaze. It makes me pause and look back at him.

"We need drinks," I blurt out and Addie laughs.

"She means truth serum. Nina will be telling us a story today about one very hot Italian stallion."

"And with that, Harrison and I are going to take Owen to play putt-putt." Jameson gets up to leave, but Harrison is still staring at me.

"H, are you coming?" Jameson is as subtle as a freight train.

"Sure. We'll be back." He seems reluctant to leave. I suppose he wants to know the sordid details of my indiscretion, but I'm glad that it'll be just George and Addie.

Our cabana boy toy, as Addie refers to him, brings our drinks along with an abundance of food. I hadn't even ordered anything, but in the middle of the table is a bottle of Patron tequila, a plate of limes, salt, and three shot glasses. Shit is getting real.

The "boy toy" pours us each a shot. I take one and then another. Enough to loosen my lips and pour out my soul. To keep my stomach happy, I get started on some smoked salmon. I don't want to get totally drunk, just numb myself while I spill my secrets.

I tell them I met Antonio at a club on the Strip while here for a trade convention where I was meeting with industry leaders in the publishing community. He was intense, hot, and magnetic. We spent the night dancing, talking, and yes, having sex. Lots and lots of sex. We were inseparable. I only went back to my room for changes of clothes. He lived in the penthouse at the hotel I was staying in and owned several clubs around the Strip. He was rich, successful, and hot. Did I say that already?

This is the hardest part to share. I close my eyes because I absolutely cannot stand to see the reaction I get when I say, "The last night of my stay, we got stupid drunk—I guess the two drinks I had were far stronger than I thought—and I woke up with a ring on my finger." It sounds even dumber when I say it out loud. I open my eyes and pour myself another shot, waiting for Addie and George to process the story.

"YOU'RE MARRIED?!" Addie's voice screeches, and the volume is at a level that dogs would probably howl to.

"Guurl ... you have some big explaining to do," George says wide-eyed. "Why would you leave your hubby here? Do you love him? Does Grammy know? This is better than any reality show I could ever watch." He takes another shot. "I wish I had some popcorn." He pops a potato skin in his mouth.

"Technically, I'm not married anymore. We annulled it within a couple of months. He didn't want to, but it wasn't love, it was lust. It was a mistake."

"I can't tell you that I'm not hurt you didn't share this with me on top of the other stuff you were holding back, but now that you've shared, what are you going to do?" Addie whispers.

"I wonder that myself, wife. What are you going to do?" I look back to find the Adonis himself, Antonio, standing next to me with his piercing chocolate eyes. Jesus. I wish my body didn't respond to him.

"I'm not your wife, Antonio. We signed the annulment papers a long time ago."

"You signed them. I did not. Didn't you wonder why you never received a finalized copy? You have been ignoring me for months. No more running. We're having dinner tonight. My penthouse at seven. Alone." His voice is commanding. Anger radiates off of him. He turns away and leaves. I suppose avoidance is no longer an option. But wait a minute … holy shit, that means I'm still married. I'm still married?! And that makes me a cheater too! I cheated on Antonio with Harrison. Is it technically cheating if I didn't know I was married?

And how could I be so stupid as to not notice I hadn't received any documents confirming our annulment? He said he'd take care of everything, and like an idiot, I believed him. Another man who let me down. I was stupid to believe him. *Stupid, stupid.*

"That was hot." Addie is fanning herself, oblivious to current freak out.

"You are still fucking married, bitch! I can't believe this. Will you be bringing him home to meet Grammy?" George's eyes dance with mischief.

Grammy. Well, that will be a lovely discussion. Maybe I'll just leave the country. Fall off the face of the Earth. Is there a witness protection program for women who find out they're still married to a virtual stranger? What happened to the mantra, "What happens in Vegas stays in Vegas"?

Addie grabs my hand and squeezes it. "Look, I can see you're confused. It's going to be okay. Someday, we'll sit back and laugh about it."

"It's going to be okay? How? What the hell am I going to do?"

"I would at least hit that one more time before you make a decision," George says.

Addie fist-bumps him, and they laugh. I'm so glad that my misery provides such excellent entertainment. My friends are super helpful.

Harrison

"**H**arrison, it's your turn. Pay attention," Owen bellows again. You see, I haven't been in the headspace to play putt-putt. I'm still thinking about Nina and what she shared last night as Olive. I sigh and take my turn. I promptly miss the easy putt and hear my cohorts snicker.

"You suck." That comment I expected from Owen, but this time it's Jameson.

"I didn't know this was a PGA championship," I snap.

"Woah, what's got your tighty-whities in a bunch? Oh wait, it's Nina. You're jelly of the Italian stallion." He laughs at his own phrasing.

"You've been with Addie too long."

He shrugs. "Well, that may be, but that Italian stallion got me some incredible action …"

I hold up my hand. I don't need or want to hear about his sex life, especially if it was inspired by Antonio. The name tastes like bile on my tongue.

I turn to Jameson as Owen plays the next hole and ask, "What would you do if you knew something about someone that they didn't know you knew?"

"What?" Confusion blankets his face.

"Imagine having a conversation with said person. They share information with you, but they don't know it's you."

His expression of "what the fuck are you talking about" is clear. How do I explain this without giving up the fact that I'm on a dating app and my match is Nina?

I blow out a breath.

"I have no clue what that rambling was about, but I think you need to talk to Nina. Be clear with your feelings. Stop this dance. You're terrible at it."

"Are you guys playing or what?" Owen glares at us.

"Sorry, Owen." I hit my shot and miss again.

"If you're having girl trouble, you should tell her she is hot and give her flowers. Girls like that," Owen states. This guy has more game than me.

"Duly noted, Casanova. I'll take that under advisement."

"I don't know who Casanova is, but I do know how to get the girls. I can be your wingman because you are terrible as mine." He sticks out his tongue and Jameson laughs. Owen turns back to the last hole and sinks his shot. "I win, losers!" He puts his fingers in the shape of an "L" on his forehead and does a little victory dance.

Right now, I really do feel like the biggest loser of all.

Nina

After my tequila buzz and soaking up rays all day, I head back to the penthouse to shower and dress for dinner. The dreaded dinner with my apparent husband. Seriously. How the hell am I going to get out of this mess? George offered to help me get ready, but I know he would pick some hot little number because his solution is to "hit it one more time." I can't. While there is a definite attraction, I think Antonio wants more than that, and my heart doesn't belong to him. I need to find an outfit that covers me up.

I'm busy throwing items of clothing on my bed in disgust when a voice says, "What did those clothes do to you?"

"Jesus, Harrison!" I shout. "You scared the shit out of me."

"Sorry. You were just so intent on a cage match with your clothes, I was interested in seeing who would win." He grins.

God, he's hot and makes my heart flip. I shake my head in an effort to rid my mind of those thoughts. *One problem at a time, and you are married for God's sake.*

"Oh, just trying to find something to wear for tonight." I don't make eye contact. How can I tell him I'm married? Will he believe me I didn't know? And the whole Captain Morgan situation is complicated on top of this one. I need to rectify this situation before I meet him. When did my life become such a soap opera?

"Jameson is excited about taking us to that new steak place on the Strip."

"Uh, yeah, well I'm not going to dinner with you all tonight. I'm having dinner with Antonio. Unfortunately." I continue foraging through my clothes.

"Oh okay. Where is he taking you?" He sounds a bit annoyed, but he's obviously trying to hide it.

"Um, his penthouse," I whisper.

"Sounds intimate."

I have to tell him. It isn't fair not to. Captain Morgan would probably agree with the sentiment, too.

"Not really. We have some things to discuss in private," I state.

"Nina, what's going on? You seem distracted and upset. I—"

I interrupt him and blurt, "I'm married. Antonio is my husband."

Harrison stares at me. His mouth opens and closes like a fish. I wait for a response.

"Did you just say you're married?"

I nod.

"Were you married … while we were in Italy?"

I can't bear to do anything but nod again.

"And you didn't tell me?" His voice is starting to rise.

"I didn't know!" I scream in frustration. "It's a Vegas cliché, but we had spent the whole weekend together. The last night we got drunk and apparently participated in a marriage ceremony. I left the next day. We agreed to annul it. I signed the paperwork and sent it to him, only he didn't sign it. I should have followed up with him, but I was so caught up with Addie's drama with her father and Owen being hit by that car, I totally forgot."

"You forgot. You forgot to follow up on the little fact that YOU ARE MARRIED?"

Are you fucking kidding me? He's screaming at me. Sure, I get it. He's mad that he didn't know, but I didn't either. Okay, yes, I dropped the ball. Perfectly organized Nina didn't follow up with Antonio. Yes, I ignored his messages, but only because I wanted to forget how reckless I was that weekend.

"Look, I understand why you're angry. I messed up, but it wasn't intentional. I'm not a cheater. And anyway, how do you think I feel about it?" I shake my head in disgust at myself.

"You have no idea why I'm upset, Nina. Good luck tonight. I hope you get everything you want."

He walks out of my bedroom, and I'm confused as to what just happened. I assume that he's upset over me being married and having sex with him in Italy, but then why would he say, "you have no idea why I'm upset"? I'm exhausted over the confusing messages the male species keeps sending me.

This is exactly why I don't do relationships. Men are infuriating and difficult. Maybe I'll just become a nun.

Harrison

W̲ell, that was surprising news. All I did was go in to see how Nina was, since I wasn't present for the conversation earlier with Addie and George. I was hoping that she would confide in me as Harrison and not Captain Morgan, but I got more than I bargained for, and I'm none too pleased about it.

Married? Fucking married. I pace back and forth. I swear I'm going to wear a hole in this carpet. My brain can't wrap itself around the concept of my Nina being committed to another man. Oh, that's right, she isn't mine. We've screwed up that option more times than I can count. How could she be so irresponsible? And the reality is that Antonio obviously wants it to work—why else would he not sign the paperwork? I shake my head in frustration.

My phone pings and I see it's a message from Olive. Fan-fucking-tastic. Now I have to act compassionate and understanding. Or not. I can easily break this off and rid myself of the anguish.

Olive: Are you available to chat tonight?

I pause. I really want to say no, but this might give me some other details that I might not get otherwise. Was this the secret my father was referring to? I can't imagine a marriage would ruin her business, but what if there's more to it? No, I need to put my own anger aside and look out for her. This is Nina, the girl who has basically owned me since she was seventeen.

Me: Sure. What time?
Olive: I have dinner plans at 7, so I was thinking 10?

Wow, ten. That means she really has no plans on staying with him. A smug smile draws across my face.

Me: Sounds good. Oh, and Olive, thank you for being so vulnerable last night. It really meant a lot to me.

I am not blowing smoke up her ass, I really valued her honesty even if she doesn't know she shared so much of herself with me. Maybe someday that can be us, but right now, this is all we have.

Nina

I head to Antonio's penthouse at the Bellagio. Oh, you want to know what I decided to wear? Well, I opted for some dressy jeans and a black, silk blouse paired with some platform sandals. I wanted simple so I don't appear as if I'm trying too hard, because I'm not. I'm simply trying to get my life back. Despite the holy hotness Antonio exudes, he isn't my soulmate. Sure, our physical chemistry is off the charts, but there isn't any real substance there, and I need to rectify this for both our sakes.

My pits are a sweaty mess, which makes me annoyed that I decided on a silk blouse. Rookie mistake. The concierge buzzed up to his penthouse and, when given confirmation of my visit, ushered me to the elevator that would lead me to Antonio's penthouse. The doors open directly into his home where he stands with a sexy smirk, dressed in tight, charcoal dress pants and a crisp, white button-down with a peek of his dark chest hair showing. Sweet. Baby. Jesus.

"Come in, Nina. Make yourself at home, since this is technically your home as my wife." He hands me a glass of champagne and gives me a soft peck on the lips. My body needs to take a back seat right now and my head needs to be in charge.

I accept the bubbly goodness and remind myself not to chug it. Alcohol got me into this situation to begin with, so I need to be very careful tonight.

"Antonio, I'm only your wife because you neglected to sign the paperwork for our annulment."

"And you neglected to answer my texts or phone calls, so I think we're even. Now, how about some dinner and conversation." He gestures with his hand to usher me toward the large table set for a romantic dinner. I shake my head in disbelief. He pulls the chair out for me and settles into the seat next to me.

"I ordered your favorite. Lobster ravioli and those yeast roles you love." He removes the silver dome from my dish and there is the most delectable meal I've seen in a while. If I were in a different emotional state, this would be heaven, but my stomach is twisted, and my appetite is nonexistent.

"Antonio, this is a lovely gesture, but we need to talk ..."

He puts his finger to my lips. "We will talk as we eat, Nina. Food is the connection to the soul."

Was he always so deep or was I caught up in the lust of the weekend?

I force myself to take a bit of the creamy concoction and close my eyes to enjoy the flavors. When I open them, Antonio is grinning at me.

"I love how you enjoy food. You savor it. It was one of the things that attracted me to you."

"You know I don't eat like this all the time, right? I am a huge health nut and my best friend, Addie, is always getting on my case for my lack of processed food intake." I give him a small smile.

"I do know that, but I love that when you indulge you enjoy it. Now, tell me about your friends."

We settle into a relaxing conversation, and I tell him everything about Addie and Jameson. I share my intense love for Owen and how grateful I am to have this tribe of people. I don't mention Harrison because, honestly, I don't know what we are to each other. Friends? Enemies? It's complicated.

We finish dinner and settle on the plush sectional facing each other. He grabs my hand and strokes my fingers with his thumb. I take back my hand and he frowns.

"We need to talk about proceeding with the annulment."

"Nina, I don't think we're on the same page. I want to talk about staying married. There is something between us and I think we should explore it."

Why does he want to stay married? He doesn't even know me. What if he won't let me go? What happens then? *Breathe, Nina.*

"Antonio, we had a wonderful weekend together and you are an amazing man, but I don't want to stay married to you. It was a mistake."

Sadness overwhelms his eyes. "All I ask is that you think about it. I know you're leaving tomorrow, but I want to get to know you better. We've done this completely backwards, but there is something between us, Nina. You can't deny it."

"I need to go, Antonio. Please just sign the paperwork so we can move on with our lives." I get up to leave and go to give him a peck on the cheek. He turns his head at the last minute and catches my lips full on, setting my desire on fire. It's so hard to pull away, but I have to. I have to control this.

"Just think about it. Please," he begs.

I press the button for the elevator and it arrives quickly. The doors open and I step in and turn around to face him.

"Goodbye, Antonio. I wish you happiness and love."

I know this is the right thing to do, but why do I feel so shitty?

Harrison

D inner with this group is always entertaining, but I can't seem to focus on the conversation. My eyes have settled on the empty chair next to me. My mood is starting to tank, and before you know it, Addie calls me out for it.

"Harrison, you know we love you, but honestly, your contribution to this conversation has been lackluster at best. In fact, if I gave you a Yelp review, it would be a one-star rating." She tilts her head at me.

Jameson and Owen are playing some game on their phones and laughing, completely oblivious to my despair, while George is checking out the bartender serving patrons nearby.

"I'm sorry. Really, I am. This is your weekend, and I'm not in the best mood. I am ..." I search for the words but find myself at a loss.

Addie grasps my hand and says, "I get it, H. I really do. We are all in shock over Nina's news, but I know her, and this is a blip. A gigantic blip with ramifications, but she will get it rectified. There's something between you two, and it would be super helpful if you just had a totally open, honest conversation. God, I have never seen two people communicate so ineffectively."

I laugh and she points her finger at me. She continues, "Grow some balls, man, and make her hear you."

"Don't you think I've tried? I have. But this marriage thing has really thrown me. I just don't know where to go from here."

"Look, Nina is berating herself for dropping the ball on this, and honestly, she doesn't need us weighing in with our opinions of the situation. What she needs is our support. Be there for her. She needs us. She needs you."

"I don't know if that's true, Addie, but I hear you."

She pats my hands and Owen says, "Food is here. Stop the meeting and let's start eating." Everyone laughs. Only Owen could bring me back to the present like that. Nina can wait. I need to celebrate with my friends.

Nina

It's 9:45 p.m. and I'm back in my hotel room. I begged off going to the club with Addie and the rest of the group. While I feel bad about abandoning ship during their weekend celebration, Addie got that I wasn't in the mood for … anything at all. And let's face it, that group would have bludgeoned me with questions I don't have answers to.

I change into my pajamas and wash the makeup off my face. It's funny that the conversation I'm about to have with Captain Morgan has me more twisted than dealing with my husband issue. Maybe it's because he demonstrated such compassion last night.

I hate hurting my friends, especially Harrison. While our relationship has always been complicated, I care about him, and my actions, even unintentionally, hurt him. I guess that shows he cares about me in a different way than I thought. But that is a conversation for another day.

I log on to the app, hoping that Captain Morgan has logged on as well. My heart flutters a bit as I see his name, but then I realize that what I'm about to tell him could change whatever this is we've been building.

Me: Hey.

Captain Morgan: Hey, yourself. Good night?

Me: It was interesting. You?

Captain Morgan: It was fine. Celebrating with friends. I have a feeling that you have something more on your mind that you want to share. What is it, Olive?

Me: Okay. Well, I just want to say that I will understand if you're angry or feel misled by me, but my disclaimer is that I didn't know.

Captain Morgan: Olive, just tell me.

Me: I'm married.

Captain Morgan: I'm confused. Tell me what happened and how you didn't know.

I tell him the story about my weekend last year with Antonio and how he didn't sign the paperwork. I admit my blunder of not following up with that and ignoring phone calls and text messages from my "spouse."

Captain Morgan: Wow, sounds like you've been through a lot in the last few days. How was the dinner tonight?

Me: Difficult. He wants to try to make it work, but I don't have that same draw to him, and I want the heart flutter.

Captain Morgan: The heart flutter?

Me: I want to be with someone who makes my heart flip and flutter. Someone who, when he walks into the room, I only see him. My only problem is me. Captain Morgan, I am a mess of epic proportions. That's the honest truth. You probably should find another person to chat with—I don't think I'm what you're looking for at this point.

Captain Morgan: I am my own worst critic. Don't you think you should forgive yourself and move forward? Sure, I'm surprised at this news, but we all make mistakes. Error is judgement simply being human. I once embarrassed a girl and hurt her terribly. Even though she hasn't forgiven me, I have forgiven myself. It's the only way to walk through the pain.

Captain Morgan is insightful, patient, and extremely kind. Wow. I feel so comfortable talking with him, and without judgement. How refreshing.

Me: You are a better person than me. I have a big mess to clean up and a tour of apologies to be made. Thank you for hearing me out and I will totally understand if this—us meeting to chat—will no longer work for you.

Captain Morgan: Not on your life. You are very colorful, and I'm enjoying getting to know you. Don't be so hard on yourself. Happy to be your friend until you get your marriage stuff worked out, of course. Then we can go from there.

Me: Oh, okay. Thank you for being so kind about this. I'll be back at my grammy's tomorrow. Do you have time to chat this week? I have my high school reunion on Friday. Something I'm dreading, but I can be flexible with my time.

Captain Morgan: You might have a better time than you think at your reunion. Anyway, I'm pretty flexible next week. How about Wednesday? Same time?

Me: That works great. Maybe you can give me a pep talk before the reunion.

Captain Morgan: I would be happy to. Goodnight, Olive. I hope you sleep well.

Me: Goodnight, Captain.

I close the chat and smile. There is something about Captain Morgan. It's the first time in a while that I've felt the urge to open up to somebody. Probably has something to do with the behind-the-screen thing, but nevertheless, I felt safe sharing with him, and that, my friends, is nothing to ignore.

Harrison

Never in my life have I been on edge about a conversation. Frankly, I was a little scared that Nina was going to make an effort with her "spouse." I use quotes because it isn't real. She doesn't love him, but I can have empathy for the guy. After all, once you know Nina, it's hard to let her go. She is strong, vibrant, but also frightened of feeling. I only wish that she knew the truth. That it's me she feels safe with and not some random guy. I just need to tell her the truth. Will I lose her or will she see that we need to give us a real chance? I shake my head.

I leave my room to get a drink of water from the kitchen, and there, in the moonlight, stands Nina. She gazes out the window, lost in her own thoughts. I could easily go back to my room without her noticing, but like a magnet, I am drawn to her.

"Nina, are you okay?"

She turns toward me, her eyes wet with tears. "I will be. Once everything is finalized with Antonio and this mess is cleared up. I will be okay." She says it like she's trying to convince herself.

"Listen, I want to apologize to you. I'm so sorry for the way I reacted to your news this afternoon. It was just a shock and I behaved terribly. Do you forgive me?"

"Of course. Do you forgive me? It was never my intent to hurt you." Her eyes beg for absolution.

"Of course I forgive you. You know I'm here for you if you need to talk."

"Am I crazy to proceed with dissolving this marriage?"

I remain silent, or more like speechless. She continues.

"He wants to make it work. He wants to try. He's the only person who has chosen me. Wants to be with me, and I'm letting him go. My whole life, people, aside from Grammy, have tossed me aside and left me, but this man wants *me*, to the point that he didn't annul our marriage just for the possibility that we could work it out." She turns away and resumes gazing out the window.

I know that I'm one of those people she's referring to. I left her. I didn't see her value and I regret that every single day, but that's in the past. I need to show her that she's enough. I'm starting to understand what Addie was talking about earlier, about showing her I see her.

"Nina, as one of the people guilty of discarding you, I'm full of regret. I allowed outside influences to manipulate my actions, and for that I'm deeply remorseful. I value you, Nina. You are an important person in my life. And while we can't seem to get on the same page in terms of how we stand with each other, I hope that one day we can. Antonio may want to try with you, but that isn't enough to fully invest. You have to want that too, Nina. Don't settle."

She turns to me and grins. One of her smiles that lights up the room. "Well, well, well, that was an amazing speech with lots of warm fuzzy feelings. I'm honored that you shared it with me."

"I meant every word, Nina. Regardless of what happens between us, we will always be connected, and I'm here for you."

When I say that, I mean it. Even though it would probably break me to see her commit to someone else, I would still want to be in her life. Whatever the capacity.

Her phone buzzes. She looks down at her screen to identify the source. She laughs, which makes my heart flip.

"It's Addie. I'm sure she wants the details of tonight, so I'd better get it over with. I don't want her to badger me on the plane home. Thanks for the talk, Harrison. I appreciate your honesty."

She turns and walks back into her room, shutting the door behind her. I'm left wondering what my next step should be and when I should come clean about Captain Morgan. Oh, the tangled web I've woven.

Nina

Since I spilled my guts to Addie last night, the plane ride back to my hometown was quiet. It might be that Addie was a tad hungover, along with George. Jameson was his usual stoic self, while Owen subtly berated Harrison for not opting to be his wingman last night. This group is a hot mess.

I texted Antonio before I left but did not hear back from him. I'm sure he's hurt. He isn't a man who gets told no very often. If things were different—if I were different—then maybe our union would be what I'm looking for, but the timing isn't ideal. I need to be okay with me, and my trust issues run deep. I exhale. My next uncomfortable task will be sharing my indiscretion with Grammy. Ugh. While she won't be mad at me, her disappointment will be evident, and that is the last thing I want her to feel. She has been my constant, and the thought of her being let down by me breaks my heart.

The limo drops me off at Grammy's and I bid farewell to my crew of merry friends. Jameson and George are headed back to New York, while Addie and Owen are extending their stay. I'm glad. Those two bring a whole lot of joy and fun to my life.

I haul my bags into the house, declining the offered assistance from Harrison. After last night's heart-to-heart, I can't risk talking to him right now. I'm too vulnerable. He makes me feel stuff that I'm not prepared for, and I thought I had stuffed that shit way down deep.

"Grammy, I'm home," I shout as I struggle with my heavy luggage.

I know she's here since I saw her car, but maybe she's out for a walk. As I get to my room, her bedroom door opens. Her cheeks are flushed and her hair is mussed. She's wearing a bathrobe at three o'clock in the afternoon.

"Are you sick? What's wrong?" She's never ill. Fear rushes through me This woman is the poster child for good health. But then I have a revelation. She isn't sick, she's getting some action. OH. MY. GOD.

"Well, you're back early," she states.

"When you fly private, you can make your own schedule. Jameson and George needed to get back to New York. You, my sweet Grammy, are avoiding an explanation."

"I am not avoiding anything. There's a lovely gentleman who has been giving me lots of attention this afternoon, and you interrupted by coming home early." She slyly grins at me.

Grammy has game. Who knew? Apparently not me. I could have gone my whole life not knowing anything about her sex life.

"On that note, I'll make myself scarce. You and your friend continue your fun. And please, let's never speak of this again."

"Oh, and sweet girl, I can already tell that you're avoiding telling me something, as well. We can talk tonight."

I pause. Damn. She always knows when I'm hiding something.

I grab my purse and head out the door while she laughs. I text Addie, "Headed your way. Grammy is 'entertaining,' and before you ask, don't."

She texts back, "You know when you tell me not to do something, I generally do it."

I shake my head and laugh. I guess I'll have to distract her with chocolate.

Nina

I walk into the Waterfall B&B and am greeted by my delightful assistant and Mason. Wait. Back up. I grin.

"Just the person I was hoping to find. You've been mysteriously silent this weekend, which is very odd, but I guess this explains some things."

Lillie grins at me and Mason scowls.

"Mason has been kind enough to show us around your quaint little town. Besides I thought you could use a break from work since you had your own situation to work out in Vegas. I told you I wouldn't contact you, remember?" She tilts her head at me. Mason studies me intently. Did Paul Revere ride through town and announce my marriage? I ignore her and turn to Mason.

"So, you've been showing Lillie and Maddie the town. That was so nice of you." I grin at him. He scoffs at me.

"It's customary to be hospitable when one has guests."

Ah, yes, but it isn't for him since he hardly socializes at all. This is a huge step for him. Lillie is glowing and smiling. It's a very good look on her.

"Where is sweet Maddie?" I inquire.

"She's hanging out with Addie and Owen. Mason wanted to take me out for a bit." She blushes. Well, aren't these two the cutest? I could get a cavity from all the sweetness.

"Well, go enjoy yourselves." I grin at them.

"Do you want to meet tomorrow morning to go over the week?" Lillie shifts to work mode in an instant.

"Sure. Why don't you and Maddie come to Grammy's for breakfast around eight? We can go over the schedule, and feel free to tell me that I need to go back to New York and miss the reunion."

"Not a chance. In fact, Mason asked me to go with him."

"Oh, really? Well, you must be a unicorn because Mason couldn't even commit to going with me."

"You can go with us," Mason interjects. That's adorable. I can't fault him since he's stepping out of his comfort zone, something I have been hoping he would do.

"Well, that would be lovely, but I think Addie is going to be my date. She insists on going with me. Something about *cutting those bitches* who bullied me." I laugh.

At that moment, I notice that Mason has grabbed Lillie's hand, and a sly grin has spread across her face. This is making my heart smile.

"You kids go have fun! I'm going to get some hugs from your sweet Maddie."

"See you tomorrow, Nina. Oh, and you know everything is going to work out, right?"

"That's the plan." I give her a smile that I hope is convincing. I watch them walk off and my own issues get pushed aside as I relish in my cousin and his huge leap. He put aside his discomfort for her. I want that.

Harrison

The whole weekend was a mindfuck. Plus, I ignored excessive texts from my father and Melanie. I didn't tell anyone where I had gone, but as you can imagine in this small town, they knew I was with Nina. But now that I know her secret, I can't imagine how this would impact her business. She would not be the first person to have a marriage mishap in Vegas.

I head to my room, lost in thoughts of Nina, her marriage, and my chats with "Olive." In fact, I'm so lost that I almost miss the hardened face of my father, waiting for me in the hallway at the B&B.

"Father."

"Well, did you enjoy your time in Vegas?"

"You don't really care about my trip. Just state your business and leave." I unlock the door to my room and usher him inside. The hallway has ears.

"You're right. I don't care. What I do care about is how you're fucking up my life by not marrying Melanie. I'm not asking you to do anything monstrous, I'm asking you to marry an attractive woman of the same social status. This merger is the financial security that our family needs." His face is flushed with rage.

"Your emergency is not my emergency," I state flatly.

He laughs. I cock my head and say, "You find that funny, old man?"

"I find it humorous that you believe that shit. It doesn't matter what you want. I will ruin Nina if you don't comply. I know you don't want that to happen, do you?"

"I already know her secret, so there's really nothing left to hold over me; plus, her sham of a marriage isn't enough to ruin her."

"For such a shrewd businessman, you are stupid. Have you looked into Antonio Rossi? Trust me. It will ruin her."

I process what he's saying and realize that I dropped the ball in not getting the 411 on that guy. He puts his hand on my shoulder. If we had a close father-son relationship, it would appear affectionate, but this is a power move.

"Look, you don't have to be in love with Melanie. Go through the motions. You can have Nina on the side. After all, that's really all she's good enough for." He smirks, heads for the door, and leaves.

I grab my phone and call Jameson immediately. I need all hands on deck to find out about Antonio Rossi ASAP.

Nina

As I make my way to Addie's room, I'm still processing Lillie and Mason. The smile on my face is genuine, and I couldn't be more pleased with my indirect matchmaking skills. She is exactly what I hoped Mason would find. I'm basking in a bit of euphoria when I literally run into Harrison's father.

"Nina, it's so good to see you! My, you certainly look amazing! It's been, what, fifteen years?"

He cocks his head as if he doesn't know the answer, but he does. He was a big part of me leaving this town earlier than I planned.

"Mr. McCall, what a surprise. I *would* say it's a pleasure to see you, but we know that's a lie." I smirk.

"Wow, Nina Bryant has a bite these days. Who would have thought? You've come a long way from the white trash you were. But as they say, once trash, always trash."

"Don't think that's a saying, but if you're congratulating me on my successful career and how far I've come, I don't really need your praise."

"Oh, don't worry, I won't be congratulating you on anything but your nuptials. Antonio Rossi is quite a catch. You've done well, but that's no surprise—you were always a gold-digging whore."

Okay. I can deal with a lot, but being called a whore is really uncalled for, so I react and punch him. Yeah, that's right, I punched him square in the face. It was liberating and quite painful. My hand is throbbing, and his look of surprise is wiped away by sheer anger.

"Bitch!" he shrieks as he cradles his face. I guess I have a mean right hook. I don't think I'll be heading to the boxing circuit, but it's nice to know I can do it if needed.

Before this evil bastard can react, Harrison swoops in and grabs his father by the arm. He is seething, and friends, not going to lie, it's hot. So hot it makes me forget that my hand might be broken.

"Get the fuck out, old man, and don't come back!" Harrison shouts.

"I'm going to have her arrested for assault," he bellows as he stumbles out the door.

Harrison turns to me with a concerned look on his face and says, "Remind me not to piss you off." He steps closer to me. "I am so sorry about my father. He's out of control. I was actually coming to find you. Let's go back to my room. You need some ice, Rocky."

"Okay," I whisper. The adrenaline is wearing off and I feel a little unsteady. Harrison wraps his arm around me and cradles me against his chest.

"It's all going to be fine. I'll make sure of it."

Harrison

I was approaching the lobby when I heard raised voices. Hearing Nina rail on my father made my feelings deepen for her. That woman is strong and unafraid. I love it. But then he called her a whore, and all bets were off. I was overcome by the need to protect her—I wasn't about to let him talk to her that way. I stormed down the hallway to find that she didn't even need me. I'm not going to lie. Watching Nina punch him was one of the hottest things I have ever experienced. She is constantly surprising me. She's fierce, and I'm so damn proud. My father's reaction was only going to escalate, so I needed to step in and diffuse the situation. He is such an asshole. Such a bully.

Now that I've successfully removed my father from the lobby—and boy, did that feel good—I escort Nina to my room. She doesn't protest, which is a good sign … or maybe not. The fire in her has dimmed now, and I can only assume whatever adrenaline she felt has evaporated. Her eyes are glossy, filled with unshed tears.

I settle her in a chair next to the window and grab some ice from the minibar. Wrapping it in a towel, I gently put it on her hand. She winces. I kneel in front of her and cup her face with my free hand. Minutes pass. I can't wait any longer. I touch my lips to hers, gently at first, then more forcefully. Our tongues dance. Ice falls to the ground as she puts her hands on my face. Our breathing grows heavy as our interlude goes on longer than I dared to hope. It feels right until she says, "My life is too complicated." I hear screeching tires in my head.

"Things don't have to be complicated. Let me help you untangle yourself from Antonio."

"No. I made this mess and I need to clean it up," she states.

"Nina, sweetheart, why are you so stubborn? Let me help. Please, don't discount this. It felt right. We feel right." I sound like I'm begging because, well, I am. Never have I felt as pathetic and needy as I do right now. "Stop fighting this. When are you going to realize that we're good together?"

She looks at me with her sad eyes. "This was a mistake. We were caught up in the emotion of what happened with your father. I'm navigating an annulment and I can't have any distractions."

"Nina, the only mistake is that you keep denying you have feelings for me. If it weren't the annulment, you would have another excuse. Take a chance, Nina," I plead.

"I can't, Harrison." She takes my hand and squeezes it. Then she promptly walks out the door with no hesitation. I have spent a good majority of my life watching her walk away from me. What she doesn't understand is that I will always go after her. Always.

Nina

I stand in the hallway with my back against the wall, trying to regain some sort of composure. That kiss. Damn Harrison. He has a magic tongue. I could feel that kiss reaching all the way to my toes. Seriously. The man has some mad skills, and I've been privy to the whole package, if you get my drift. I exhale. This day has been one big shit show. Grammy is having sex. I punch Harrison's dad, and then Harrison takes my tongue hostage. I. Can't. Even.

Out of the corner of my eye, I see the two sweetest faces on the planet. Owen and Maddie are walking toward me with big grins on their faces. Excellent. I need a distraction. A good one, not the kind that involves testosterone.

Owen reaches for me and gives me a tight hug. His hugs are the best. He releases me to Maddie, who's smiling up at me.

"You two look like you're up to no good." I sign as I talk to them.

"Addie said we could go get a snack. There are cookies in the lobby. She says we can have two each, but what she doesn't know won't hurt her." He laughs. Owen is always trying to outsmart his sister. He does an excellent job of it most of the time.

"Well, I'll see you in a bit; I'm headed to your room."

"What happened to your hand?" Maddie signs.

I'm certainly not going to tell them I punched someone, so I lie. "My hand got caught in the door."

They look at me as if they know I'm full of shit, but this is my lame-ass story, and I'm sticking to it.

"Looks like you punched someone," Owen states as he gives me the stink eye.

"I would never punch anyone. Violence is never the answer." I am going straight to hell for lying to these two.

"Whatever you say, Nina. I bet you punched 'em good." He laughs and they walk off to consume massive amounts of cookies while I'm left shaking my head. I walk down the hallway and knock on Addie's door. It swings open and her eyes dance with mischief.

"Well, well, well, you certainly have been busy since you said you were on your way. I didn't realize I was besties with a prize fighter. You know the lobby is the best source of gossip." She ushers me into the room while she giggles.

I narrow my eyes at her and say, "How do you know what happened?"

"I have my ways." She wiggles her eyebrows. I shake my head in disbelief. Nothing is sacred with this group.

Nina

Addie hands me a bottle of water and we settle on her bed. "What the fuck happened?" she implores.

I dive into the story from the very beginning. I share about Grammy and her sexual exploits—cue my shudder, although I'm happy for her—along with my interaction with Mason and Lillie, which, by the way, was the highlight of my day, all the way to the fight with Harrison's father.

"And?" she asks. Addie has this uncanny ability to know when I'm holding back vital information. No wonder she and Grammy get along so well.

Sigh.

"Harrison took me back to his room and put ice on my hand."

"And?"

I clear my throat and whisper, "And he kissed me."

A big grin spreads across her face as if she's the instigator for this particular event. "Did you like it?"

"Of course I liked it, Addie. He has a magic tongue. I am very familiar with the gifts Harrison has to offer, but I can't have any distractions. My life is super complicated right now. I need to clean up this marriage matter with Antonio. We're a train wreck that has never righted itself, and …"

"Bullshit," she spits.

"Why do you say that?" I ask, even though I really don't want the answer.

"You're always making excuses because you're scared. Harrison cares about you. He was so lost in Vegas after learning about your 'marriage'. I don't think you give him any credit for the intensity of the feelings he has for you."

"The only thing we have is lust. Trust me. You can't build a relationship on that."

"You are a big, fat, phony liar. You're in love with him, but you're so scared of being hurt that you have this gigantic cement wall no one will be able to break through. You know I've been there too, and it took Owen almost dying to have my come-to-Jesus moment."

Tears form in my eyes thinking about last year and how we almost lost Owen when he was hit by a car running into traffic. He had just learned that who he thought was his father was actually a con man using him for money.

"It's a lonely existence, Nina, and I would hate for you to have regrets. You need to think long and hard about the excuses you keep handing out like candy."

I hate it when quirky Addie becomes profound, inspirational Addie because it forces me to acknowledge that no one else is the problem here. It's all me.

Nina

I head back to Grammy's, hoping that her afternoon delight, aka Marvin, has left. What a weird day. In the span of a few hours, I found out my Grammy is getting more action than me, I punched Harrison's father, and then I shared an amazing kiss with the most infuriating man. Busy day. As I open the door, I'm greeted by the aroma of pot roast. Shit. This is the meal she always used to coerce information out of me, and since we haven't chatted since I got home, I'm betting that she knows about my nuptials. Awesome.

As I enter the kitchen, she turns and eyes me. Then she grabs my hand and leads me to the table. "Look, I made your favorite." Her eyes sparkle. Could be from the action she got today, or perhaps she's giddy with the prospect of interrogating me. It's a toss-up.

"Yeah, I smelled your amazing cooking when I walked in, but I know your agenda, so let's eat and get this over with, please." My tone is curt, and I instantly regret it. I lean on the table. "Grammy, I am so sorry. It's been a weird day. Okay, scratch that, it has been a weird forty-eight hours, and I'm feeling a little out of sorts."

She squeezes my hand, and then serves me a plate of pot roast along with her buttermilk biscuits and sits down next to me. While

I'm not ravenous, this plate of comfort food reminds me that I'm not alone in this. We have walked through many challenges together. She is one of my people, and I know there will be no judgement with my current situation. Or rather multiple situations, because I honestly can't keep up.

"Do you want to talk about it?" she asks.

"Not really, but I probably need to lay it all out for you."

I tell her everything. The marriage. The kiss with Harrison. My chats with Captain Morgan. Oh, and punching Harrison's dad. At the end of my verbal dissertation, she gets up from her chair and pulls me into a hug. I inhale the sweet scent of lavender. She smells like a warm spring day. Comforting. Safe. I exhale as if I have been holding my breath for the last forty-eight hours.

"What are you going to do?"

"That's what I was hoping you would tell me. I trust your opinion."

"Oh no. This is your journey, my sweet girl. Trust yourself and your heart."

"I'm a hot mess." I shake my head. My heart and brain are at war with each.

"You are a *beautiful* mess, but aren't we all in some way? Go relax and get a good night's sleep. Things will be better in the morning."

While that would be a comforting statement with a normal situation, I'm pretty sure I'll still be just as confused as I am right now. I help her clean up the kitchen, then head upstairs to my bedroom. I toss my clothes on the floor and get into my pajamas. It's early in the evening, which will give me an opportunity to get some work done. That will be an excellent distraction from my current situation. I pull up a new manuscript Lillie emailed me and try my best to immerse myself in the words of this new writer. When I realize I've read the same sentence a few times, I put my laptop aside and close my eyes. My phone begins to buzz. I'm not in the mood to talk to anyone, but I change my mind when I see it's a reminder to chat on the dating app.

I need to tell him that we probably shouldn't talk anymore. It isn't fair to him or me.

> *Me: Hi.*
> *Captain Morgan: Hi. How are you? I've been thinking about you today.*

Shit. I go through a dry spell and now it's like it's raining men.

> *Me: That's sweet.*

Lame response, I know.

> *Captain Morgan: Just thought I would check in on you. I know you have had a difficult couple of days, and I just wanted you to know I'm here for you.*

Seriously, where was this guy before my life turned to shit? The timing sucks.

> *Me: Well, I appreciate that so much. It's been a weird day. Let's just sum it up by saying that if I thought things were messy yesterday, it became a shitshow today.*
> *Captain Morgan: Sounds tough. Want to talk about it?*
> *Me: Not really. I need to be honest with you about something. I know we really aren't anything but two people getting to know each other, but I kissed someone today. I just thought you should know. I mean, not that it matters because I'm currently married, and I don't want to move forward with anything until that whole situation is resolved. I'm rambling. See, I'm a hot mess. You should run and maybe find someone else.*
> *Captain Morgan: Wow, that was a lot of information. Olive, we're friends. Not that I love the idea that you kissed someone else*

or that you are currently "married." I use the quotes because let's face it, it's a formality. I still want to get to know you and support you. Trust me, I'm no saint. We're all a little messy.

Me: *That's actually what my grandmother said to me. That each of us has our own baggage and sometimes it gets messy. Thank you. You're special, Captain Morgan.*

Captain Morgan: *Tell me about the kiss, but only if you're comfortable. We're friends, and I want you to know you can trust me.*

How do I respond to that? I mean, we kind of just friend-zoned each other. Maybe a male perspective would be helpful.

Me: *This kiss was confusing. The man, Harrison, has been in my life since high school, and we've been dancing around our attraction for years. We've dabbled, but the timing never seems right.*

Captain Morgan: *So when you say the kiss was confusing, does that mean he's a bad kisser?*

Me: *Oh, no! He is an amazing kisser, it just confused me, that's all. I'm so sorry. Is this weird? We're on a dating site, yet you're counseling me on the mess that is my life. You know, I'm not everyone's cup of tea.*

Captain Morgan: *I would not have asked if it was going to make me uncomfortable. Olive, it's fine. If this Harrison person is someone you'd like to date, then maybe you should commit to seeing it through. And while you think you aren't for everyone, maybe you are for him. Maybe you're his cup of tea.*

Me: *You deserve a special woman, Captain Morgan, and I hope you find her.*

Captain Morgan: *Something tells me I will.*

Me: *Thanks for listening. Goodbye.*

Captain Morgan: *Goodbye.*

Harrison

I can't help but smile as I finish my conversation with Nina. She will put my balls in a vice grip when she finds out I'm Captain Morgan, but she finally confirmed that there is something between us. Getting through her hard shell has been nothing short of frustrating. She shuts me out every time. I know that my actions have defined her outlook on relationships, but I need to seize this moment. I need to show her that taking a chance on me, on us, will be worth it.

I pick up the phone and call Grammy. It's risky because she hasn't always been a fan, but she is fair and I know she won't filter herself when it comes to Nina.

The phone rings. I'm pacing and my nerves are like Mexican jumping beans. This could be my last hope.

"Hello."

She doesn't have caller ID. In fact, she has a retro rotary landline phone because she is definitely old school.

"Grammy, it's Harrison. I need your help."

"Finally. When did you get your head out of your ass?"

"Just a few minutes ago." I chuckle.

I tell her about the dating app and Nina's confessions to me. Grammy knows Nina probably better than anyone. She's the only person who can help me navigate Nina's heart.

"Well, Harrison, that's a lot of information. That girl is going to kick your ass for impersonating a potential dater. I know it wasn't on purpose, but once you knew it was her, you should have come clean."

I grimace. She's right, of course. My only excuse is that I was addicted. Addicted to her raw honesty with a stranger. Maybe she felt safer that way, but I want to be that person for her. I need to be that person for her.

"With that being said, I think your best course of action is to be honest with her. Do it before the reunion, and you need a grand gesture. Something that shows her that she's important to you."

"Okay. I can do that. Do you think I have a chance?"

Never in my life have I been so desperate for a woman. As dramatic as it sounds, I need her like I need air. I'm a complete goner and could kick myself over the years we've wasted.

"One more thing. You better bring your A game because her husband just showed up and he looks determined to keep her as his."

My jaw clenches at the news. "When did he show up?"

"Just now, I can see him out of the window. It must be him, he's just like Nina described him."

"Okay. I'm on my way."

We end the call. I remember something my father said about me not having all the information on Antonio, so I call Jameson to see what he and Grady have found out. I need all the ammunition I can get if I'm going to win the girl.

Nina

After everything that's happened today, I decide to get some work done. Throwing myself into my career has always been my escape. I send some emails, make some calls, and am interrupted by a knock on the front door. Curiosity seizes me and I abandon my tasks to head downstairs.

The man standing on the other side of the door is none other than my soon-to-be ex-husband. Is my life a fucking joke? What have I done to the universe to deserve this shit?

"Hello, wife." Antonio grins at me with his ridiculously perfect smile. What? I can't help it if he's gorgeous, and my body whispers, "Hey there." when he's around. But I will tell you, just between us, that my body actually *screams* when it's in the presence of Harrison. That's the difference. It has always been Harrison, and it's taken me this long to realize just how strong our pull actually is. While I'm drowning in my own thoughts, Antonio leans in and kisses me. Not an intense smoldering kiss, but more of a friendly peck on the lips.

"What are you doing here?" I'm back from thoughts of which of these two men my body responds to the most and am finally able to formulate words. Then I begin to feel self-conscious in my pajamas with donuts on them. What? Addie gave them to me as a joke and they are super comfortable. She said she couldn't find any with kale on them. She is such a comedian. And why do I care how I look anyway?

"Is that any way to greet your husband? I came to meet your grammy and see where you grew up. I want to make this work, love, I told you that. I love you."

Are you fucking kidding me right now? He doesn't love me. He loves the idea of possessing me. Nobody will possess me.

While I thought I was thinking those things, I apparently blurted them out, and his black eyes narrow at me.

"Is that what you think? You believe I want to possess you? Own you? Nina, I want to be with you. From the first moment I met you, I was drawn to you and only you. Please. Give me a chance."

My inner red flags are waving. There is something too desperate about his pleas. There's so much I don't know about him. I mean, it's not like there was a whole lot of conversation in the time we slept together; and over the last year, I've tried to forget my indiscretion. The question is, why is he so desperate to hold on to me? He can't love me. He doesn't even know me. And anyway, I'm not relationship material. My inability to get vulnerable with men is not overly attractive, as I was told by past douches.

"Antonio, what's really going on? Look, I'm not naïve enough to think you're magically in love with me. We barely know each other. Plus, who are those big men standing outside? What are you hiding?"

For the first time ever, he's scaring me. A dark shadow flashes across his face, but it's quickly replaced by a smile. A smile that doesn't reach his eyes.

"Love, those men come with me all the time. I'm a successful businessman who, like anyone else in this industry, has some enemies. Nothing special. Don't worry about them. You're always safe with me."

Timeout. I need to have a word with you all while I'm processing this information. If someone says "you're always safe with me" and you don't feel safe, you should probably pay attention to that gut feeling, right? Okay. That's what I thought. I just wanted to make sure I wasn't losing my mind.

"Antonio, I want an annulment. Sign the paperwork and we can go our separate ways. You deserve a woman who loves you, and that isn't me. I'm sure there's someone out there made for you, but you won't find her if you're searching for something with me that simply isn't there."

"Oh Nina. You are the woman for me. I'm in town for the rest of the week. We'll have dinner and discuss the logistics of our union. Until then." He leans down and kisses me again. I turn my head so his lips land on my cheek, and I remain mute because it's as if nothing I said was acknowledged. I'm in some deep trouble, and I think I need to get some help on this. That means I need Harrison.

Nina

"Where did your husband go? I didn't even get to interrogate him." Grammy snickers.

"Grammy, this isn't the time. I need to get to Harrison. I think he's the only one who can help me get out of this situation." I run and grab my keys and purse. I look down and realize that I'm in my pajamas. Maybe I should change.

"Are you alright? What did he say to you?" Concern blankets her face. I grab her hand.

"Nothing for you to worry about, Grammy. I will get this cleaned up and we'll never speak of it again. I'll be back soon."

I run upstairs, throw on some leggings and a sweatshirt, and sprint to the front door. As I run through the door, I hit a hard, fit body. I know this body, and my heart starts to race as I make eye contact. Harrison. He's here.

"I was just coming to find you," I tell him breathlessly.

"That's exactly what I have always hoped you would say to me, among other things." He smirks.

We stare at each other until I turn and look away.

He walks around me and hugs Grammy, who then excuses herself and heads to bed, but not before I witness her pat his arm and whisper, "Good luck." I feel like I'm on a reality show where everyone knows what's going on except one person. In case you're wondering, I'm playing the part of that one person who isn't in the know.

Harrison makes himself comfortable on the couch, stretching out his long legs. I sit on the edge, not sure if I want to make a run for it or not. You see, asking for help from him is a big step, and I'm so scared of how I'm feeling about him. I am a hot mess.

"So, why are you here?" I ask casually.

"Why were you on your way to find me?" he throws back.

God, we are both so stubborn.

"I was coming to find you because I need your help." I twist my hands in my lap and stare at the floor.

I share the conversation I had with Antonio. I tell him about my concerns and that my gut says he's hiding something.

"He seemed desperate, and don't even get me started on the two bodyguards he brought with him. It was just so sketchy, and I thought maybe you could help me get to the bottom of this after all so I can be rid of him."

Harrison smirks at me. "So you want my help?"

Ugh, this man is so infuriating. "Yes, I would very much like your help."

"Was that hard?" he asks.

"What?" I'm confused.

"Asking me for help. Was it hard?"

Why is he needling me now? I have half a mind to tell him to get lost.

"Yes, it was difficult to ask. Please, Harrison. I don't need you to be an ass right now. My life is a complete shitshow. I think my husband is in the mob or something, and he won't let me go." Unshed tears pool in my eyes. I don't want to cry in front of him. It's too much vulnerability. I just feel so lost and alone right now, and his attitude isn't helping.

Instead of fighting me, he hauls me onto his lap and cradles me. I inhale his woodsy, spicy scent and wrap my arms around his neck. It feels comfortable. It feels like home. We sit in compatible silence for a few moments. Why can't he always be like this?

"Nina," he whispers.

"Yeah?" I whisper back.

"After I help you, I'm going to work on winning you. I just thought you should know."

"You are?" His admission defrosts the emotional barriers I've put in place to protect my heart. I lift my head and look him in his soulful eyes.

"I am. This time you aren't going to run. If you do, I'll chase you. While you might not be for everybody, you're definitely for me."

Those words. Where have I heard those words?

His lips connect with mine and I'm lost. Our tongues tangle. My hands roam his hair. He breaks the kiss and grins.

"Looks like I have some work to do. I'll see you tomorrow."

I reluctantly remove myself from his lap. My lips tingle.

He gives me a quick kiss and walks out the door. What the hell is happening?

Harrison

Ever had the feeling of purpose? Like everything fits? That's what I feel right now. The purpose of outing Antonio and his motives. The purpose of removing him from the picture and claiming Nina as mine. Sure, I also have the task of telling her that I'm Captain Morgan, but I feel that after I clean up the Antonio situation, that will be a blip. You don't agree? Okay, you might have a point. Nina detests being lied to, but if we are being technical, I didn't even know it was her in the beginning. Do you think I'm rationalizing and justifying? Of course you do. Maybe I am. Maybe after that electrifying kiss, I simply want to skip over that part. Before I can even contemplate addressing that particular issue, I need to focus on Antonio.

I call Jameson and share the information I learned from Nina, sans the kiss. He's collaborating with Grady to find out as much as he can. So far, we know that Antonio is a successful businessman in Vegas who owns several clubs and restaurants. The rumor mill is full of stories that he has ties to the mob, but there's nothing concrete. He appears on the up-and-up, but why is he desperate to keep Nina? Don't get me wrong. Nina is a catch, but he barely knows her, and while he contacted her during their year apart, he wasn't overly persistent until now. And then there's the comment my father made to me about not knowing everything about Antonio. He practically taunted me, and that thought is gnawing at me. What connection does my father have to Nina's soon-to-be ex?

Jameson is scheduled to be back in town this week and hopes to have more information from Grady. Apparently, we are all going to the reunion together, which should be interesting since that's the last place Nina wants to be. Hell, I don't even want to be there, but I have some surprises in store for her. Hopefully I'll have all the intel on Antonio and we can move forward. It's destiny. We are meant to be together. I just need to convince her.

Nina

My lips can still feel his lips for a full ten hours after it happened, which does not help me have a restful night's sleep. I mean, I've kissed him before, and trust me, it's hot. He does great things with those lips. My whole body can't help but respond to him. I can deny it all I want, but Harrison is it. He's the one. I've been denying it for years because of all the hurt and, let's be honest, my pride was damaged. I have wasted so much time. Captain Morgan was right.

Wait … When Harrison said, "While you might not be for everybody, you're definitely for me," I felt like I was having a déjà vu moment. As if I had heard those words before, and fairly recently at that.

Oh. My. God. Could Harrison be Captain Morgan? Jesus. How stupid am I? Don't answer that. Obviously, I'm teetering on the brink of losing it since I'm married, maybe to a mob boss, and I'm completely clueless on spilling my guts to a man I thought was a stranger. Could my life be any more humiliating? I'm sure it can, I just really don't want to experience it.

My thought process is disrupted by Addie bursting through my bedroom door.

"Why did I just see your husband at the B&B?"

Jesus. It's a little too early in the morning for her interrogation, but she's adorable and a tad annoying when she's got questions. Owen is behind her, rolling his eyes. I giggle.

"Why are you laughing? Your life is starting to resemble the three-ring circus that I entertained last year. Why aren't you freaking out right now? Are you fucking glowing? What is happening?" she bellows.

"Addie is crazy. Does Grammy have any cookies?" Owen begs. He desperately wants to be removed from this situation. As if she read his mind, Grammy appears and ushers him into the kitchen. "Let's go make some cookies, Owen," she says with a big smile on her face.

"Thank God. My sister is getting on my nerves. I can't wait for Jameson to get back because she isn't as nuts with him around."

Addie glares at him.

After they leave the room, Addie stares at me and her eyes narrow. She tries to be intimidating, but let's face it, she really isn't.

"Spill it." She settles on my bed.

"Do you have the final chapters of your book ready?" I love to deflect.

"We are *not* talking about business, Nina. We are talking about the shit show exploding all over your life. It's like the universe was constipated and then took a laxative. That's what your life resembles."

"That is oddly specific and graphic. Sounds shitty." I laugh.

"This isn't funny. What the hell is going on with you? I thought I was the only one with an insane asylum-themed life."

"I didn't want you to have all the fun. Besides, it will all work out because Harrison is taking care of it." I try not to smile.

"Did you all do the nasty? Here?" She is wide-eyed and grinning.

"God no! Get your mind out of the gutter. He kissed me after Antonio left." Heat creeps up my face. Is it hot in here?

"That's awesome! Wait, please back up and tell me what's up with Antonio's appearance."

I fill her in on the events of my whole day. By the end of my torrid tale, she's laughing so hard, tears are streaming down her face.

"You know that none of this is really that funny, right?"

"Please, cool and controlled Nina loses her shit and wails on her soon-to-be lover's father while still married to a possible mobster, after she catches her grandmother getting lucky with a bingo speed-dating participant. I bow to you and am grateful because now my shit doesn't sound so nutty."

We both start laughing, and at that moment, Owen walks in and says, "Great. Addie's crazy is contagious."

Nina

Owen and Addie stay for breakfast and are joined my Mason, Lillie, and Maddie, who appear like a cozy little family. I notice the sideway glances my assistant shares with my cousin. I also notice that Mason seems more engaged than he usually is, and Maddie is talking a mile a minute with her hands. She is loving hanging out with Owen and Grammy. It feels good to have the people I love under one roof. Okay, it's missing a few people, and I will include Harrison in that collection. I'm seeing him for the man he truly is, and I think I might finally be having an emotional breakthrough that would make a therapist proud.

My phone pings and my heart beats faster. Hoping it's Harrison, I look down, only to be a tad disappointed that it's Cassie and Marley encouraging me to come to The Watering Hole for drinks tonight. That's the last place I want to be, but since I haven't seen them since the first night I arrived, I cave. We plan to meet at eight. I would rather be in my pajamas.

"Addie, Lillie, are you girls up for a night out at The Watering Hole? I'm meeting Cassie and Marley at eight."

"Hell yeah!" Addie bellows.

"Maddie really needs to get to bed early, so I think I'll pass."

"Nonsense, Owen and Maddie can hang out here," Grammy says. "I have an air mattress I can put in the living room for her. We can eat the cookies that Owen and I baked and play games. We'll have fun."

Maddie signs "please" to her mother, and Owen basically tells Addie he's staying.

"Are you sure? I don't want to impose," Lillie says.

"Of course I'm sure. I love spending time with these two. Go and have fun!"

"Alright, I'm in, Nina." She grins at me and signs to Maddie that she can stay with Grammy. Owen and Maddie jump up and down with excitement while Mason looks out of place.

"Mason, you can come, too, if you want. I mean, it is girls' night, but you've always been part of the girls group," I joke.

"Women need time to socialize together. That is their fundamental bonding time when they gossip. I think I'll go home and work on my new app." His eyes find Lillie's and she smiles softly at him.

Interesting.

"Okay, but you're missing out because I bet Addie embraces her inner karaoke diva." I laugh.

"My ears bleed when my sister sings." Owen grimaces and Addie rolls her eyes.

"I'm an undiscovered talent. Just you wait. Some bigwig music producer is going to find me one day, and you all will be jealous," she declares.

"Stick to writing, sweet friend." I chuckle and she looks offended. I love Addie, but she's tone deaf. It only gets worse with alcohol.

Nina

As I'm getting ready to leave for the bar, my phone pings and I see Captain Morgan has logged on and wants to chat. I debate whether to engage. It would be fun to mess with him. On the other hand, if it's not Harrison like I think it is, I need to nip this in the bud because my life keeps getting messier by the moment and this guy should probably exit stage left.

> *Captain Morgan: Hey.*
> *Me: Hey.*
> *Captain Morgan: How are things going?*
> *Me: I'm not sure. Today has been odd to say the least.*
> *Captain Morgan: Do you want to share? I'm happy to be an impartial*
> *   listening ear.*

I pause. I actually wish this were a stranger. It would be so easy to spill, but my wall is up because my instincts say that Harrison is the man I have grown attached to through this dating app.

Me: *Honestly, things are messy. I feel awful using you as a sounding board. It's kind of awkward since we're on a dating app. Are you sure you're okay with this?*

Captain Morgan: Olive, I am okay with whatever you're going to share.

I giggle to myself.

Me: *Honestly, there's a relationship I've been avoiding. I need to see where it goes, if anywhere. We have been doing quite a dance for over a decade.*

Captain Morgan: Aww, the infamous Harrison. I hope you make it work, Olive. You're worthy of a passionate, loving relationship. Remember when you said you aren't for everyone and I said you might be right for someone?

Me: *Yes.*

Captain Morgan: Maybe that someone is Harrison.

Bingo. I am enjoying Captain Morgan being a cheerleader for himself.

Me: *You don't even know Harrison, yet you are his biggest cheerleader. I find that refreshing. I bet this is a first for a dating app.*

Captain Morgan: It sounds like Harrison is the ideal guy for you. After all, you said that you have been dancing around each other for a decade, and now you seem to be at a good place. He has even offered to help you get out of your current situation with your spouse. I think he's a keeper.

Busted. I never told Captain Morgan how Harrison was willing to work some magic on my current situation.

Me: *I don't remember telling you that tidbit of information. In fact, I really haven't gone in-depth about how Harrison plans to help me. Care to explain?*

The chat becomes silent and I can only imagine Harrison is about to shit himself. I laugh out loud simply because of how twisted every situation I am involved in seems to get. Finally, the dots on the screen begin to dance. This should be good.

Captain Morgan: *Any chance you won't castrate me when you see me, Nina?*

Me: *Depends.*

Captain Morgan: *I didn't realize it was you until we were in Vegas, and then I couldn't stop because it was like I was really getting to know you. Like the walls were down and you were so transparent. Are you mad?*

Me: *Honestly, a little, but I get it. I loved our conversations and without knowing that we were who we were. It did allow us to be real with each other. I'm glad you are Captain Morgan. Although, the originality of the name is lacking.*

Captain Morgan: *Oh, and yours was much better? Olive, please.*

Me: *What? I love olives in my martinis. I thought it was clever.*

Captain Morgan: *Are we okay?*

Me: *Yeah. We are. Now take down your profile. We can't have Captain Morgan helping any other damsel in distress.*

Captain Morgan: *You are the only damsel I want.*

Me: *Aw, Captain Morgan is swoony. Alright, let's take our profiles down and not lie to each other ever again.*

Captain Morgan: *Agreed.*

Harrison

My grin is currently hurting my face. I couldn't be happier that Olive/Nina has decided that our relationship is worthy of pursuing. I think she has moved past the anger. Hopefully, she'll forgive me. I seem to apologize a lot to her.

Addie texted me to let me know they're headed to The Watering Hole. She has been an excellent wing woman and cheerleader. She knows how stubborn Nina can be and is going out of her way to help me. Although she did threaten castration if I hurt Nina again. Duly noted.

I head out with renewed energy. The walk to The Watering Hole is short, although I could walk for miles with the mood I'm in. I open the door to the already crowded space. Thursday nights tend to attract a larger group, probably because there's nothing else this town offers; plus, it's karaoke night. I scan the bar looking for my prey and I spot her. She's laughing at something Addie is saying. I love her laugh, her smile, and even her sass. As if she feels me looking at her, her eyes meet mine, and her glow brightens.

Addie sees me and waves me over, but Nina whispers something to her and Addie nods. Nina rises from her seat and heads toward me. She smiles at me, and it's the smile that I like to refer to as "happy Nina." I love the happy Nina smile.

"Drink?" She gestures at the bar and I nod in agreement. We find a space and I motion to the bartender.

"What can I get you?" He eyes Nina and she grins.

"I would love rum and coke. Please make it with Captain Morgan. Oh, and make it a double." She turns to me and smiles with her eyebrow raised.

I have a feeling this will be a running joke between us for the rest of our lives.

"Actually, the lady would prefer a dry martini with top-shelf gin and two olives."

The bartender looks confused, but Nina confirms that she would rather have the martini, while I just go with whatever beer they have on tap.

"So, Captain Morgan. Are we done role-playing?"

I lean closer to her. We are almost nose to nose, and I say, "The only role-playing I would like to engage in would be in the bedroom."

"Don't change the subject, although that does sound interesting, but it doesn't change the fact that you deceived me." The slight sound of hurt in her voice slays me.

"You're right. I did, and for that, I am sorry. I do think it helped us get where we are now though. We're so good together. Don't you see? We've wasted so much time allowing outside entities to disrupt us. I thought after Italy we were finally going to move forward, but then you shut down when we got home."

"I thought you only wanted sex. I didn't know you wanted a relationship. You never said anything."

We are two of the most stubborn people on the planet. All this time and we both wanted the same thing.

"You're right. I didn't say anything because I was convinced you couldn't forgive me for the past. Look, we're both to blame for this. I apologize for my part in the whole dating app debacle. I never meant to deceive you, but I'm happy that you want to move forward with me."

She grins at me and says, "I'm actually glad you were Captain Morgan, so I forgive you. Now, how about a kiss?"

Our lips are just about to touch when a voice shouts, "Why the fuck are you about to kiss my wife?"

Our heads turn at the same time. We both take a step back at the sight of my father, Melanie, and Antonio.

Fuck. My. Life.

Nina

So fucking close to having a tongue tango with Harrison, and in walk the three stooges. Seriously. While I'm absorbing their arrival, it doesn't escape my attention that these three seem awfully familiar with each other, standing so close together and appearing at exactly the same time. Things that definitely make you go "Hmmm …"

While I love a good alpha-male stare down, I opt to wiggle my way in between them. Melanie pokes her bony finger in my face as she screams, "You whore! You're married and cheating with my fiancé." This bitch is exhausting. We have now captured the attention of the whole bar. I would like to point out that this situation is probably the most exciting thing to happen since they installed the sole traffic light over twenty years ago. Anyway, I see Addie, Cassie, Lillie, and Marley move to surround us.

"Excuse me!" I bellow. The chatter in the bar ceases and our interaction is center stage. The power of silencing people is my gift. "Melanie, let me set the record straight. You are not engaged to Harrison, I'm annulling my accidental marriage to Antonio, Harrison and I are finally together. Now march your dumb ass back to whatever hellhole you are currently living in and leave us the alone."

I hear Addie squeal behind me. Guess that means she's happy for us.

"Pretty sure of yourself for white trash, aren't you, Nina?"

I look at Lyle. His distinguished face is now adorned with black and blue due to my fantastic punch. He seems so confident. I wonder what bullshit he's touting.

"Yep." I pop the P for emphasis. "And if you're so desperate for a man, you can have *my* trash—I'm done with him." I nod at Antonio, whose eyes sear into me.

"I have information that could destroy your business and your life. In fact, Nina, your whole life is really a lie. Just another chess piece that I enjoy maneuvering. Honestly, you and Harrison would never be a formidable couple because despite your success, you're nothing but trash. Disposable, worthless trash." He sneers.

There are moments in life when you either cower or you rise. I'm not sure how this is going to go, but I know that I'm done running. But before I can utter a word, Addie's phone rings. I hear her panicked voice telling the person on the other end that we'll be right there. My heart sinks because I know it's Grammy. Call it instinct, but before Addie says anything, I look in her eyes and say, "Let's go."

Our group pushes past the assembly of idiots and heads out the door. Harrison grabs my hand and I let him. I need him. Grammy has got to be okay. We get in Marley's car and I turn to Addie. "What happened?"

"Owen said that Grammy said she had a headache, went to take some pain relievers, and then fell down. He called 911. The paramedics got there, and Maddie and Owen went with them."

Lillie is crying. "I should have been there with her. I hope she's not scared."

I grab her hand. "Don't worry, Lillie. Owen will watch over her until we get there."

"Oh Nina. You don't need to comfort me. I know Owen will take good care of her. I'm so grateful; this is the closest experience I've ever had to family. You and Grammy and your friends. I feel like I'm no longer alone. Your grammy has become so important to me in such a short time. I just want her to be okay."

"She's a fighter." I can't say anything more because the dam is about to burst. That woman is my everything. She is my home, my support, and my number one fan. I've failed her by putting my petty resentments about this town ahead of visiting more. If anything happens to her, I don't know that I can forgive myself.

"Hey," Harrison whispers in my ear. "She's a badass and so is her granddaughter. She's going to be okay. She'd never allow anything less." He squeezes my hand and kisses the side of my head. His strength is what I need, and I can't believe I wasted so much time thinking otherwise.

Time is sparse and fleeting. From this point on, I'm going to be mindful of that very thought. We pull up to the hospital and get out of the car. I send up a silent prayer. Not sure who that will go to, as I'm not an overly spiritual person, but I'm hopeful someone will hear me.

Harrison is still holding my hand as we approach the front desk. The last time I was in a hospital was when Owen got hit by a car and we weren't sure if he would make it. I shake the thought from my head. "I'm looking for Catherine Lloyd. She was brought in by ambulance."

"Are you family?" she inquires.

"Yes, I'm her granddaughter."

"Okay, hon. Let me get the doctor. Just have a seat over there and someone will be with you shortly."

Our group makes its way over to a group of chairs. A volunteer is sitting with Owen and Maddie. Both are visibly shaken. Lillie and Addie head over to them without pause and embrace them, whispering words of comfort. Owen breaks from Addie's tight hug and runs to me. I open my arms and Owen almost knocks me over with his fierce warmth. He leans his head back and says, "Nina, I was so scared, but I remembered what Addie taught me and called for help. I hope she's going to be okay. I love her. She's what I hoped a grandmother would be like."

"Oh Owen. You did a great job. Grammy is so lucky you were there." I smile through my unshed tears. "I'm so very proud of you and she will be, too. She loves you. I promise we'll come back a lot to visit her from now on."

"That would be fun. Can we bring Maddie? She was scared, but I helped her." He puffs out his chest and I can't help but giggle at him.

"You did great, Owen," Harrison says, clapping a hand on his shoulder. "No one could've done better than you did."

"I'm grateful you were there for them. I love you so much, Owen."

"I love you too, Nina, even if you want Harrison to be your boyfriend." He rolls his eyes and I give him another squeeze. He heads over to Addie, probably begging for money to go raid the vending machine. Lillie is cradling Maddie in her lap. Marley and Cassie are holding each other's hands. These are my people, and I couldn't be more fortunate to have them in my life.

"Do you need anything?" Harrison asks.

"No, thank you. I'm okay. Once things calm down, we need to talk about what happened tonight."

"I know. I have Jameson working with Grady to find out what Antonio is hiding. Once we find out how Grammy is, I'll call Jameson and relay what happened at the bar. My father is definitely the orchestrator to this insanity. Actually, I wouldn't be surprised if Addie summoned Jameson here."

I see the doctor walking toward us. His face is serious and his stride is quick. He approaches the group and asks, "Is there a Nina Bryant here?"

"That's me. How is my grandmother?"

He gives me a soft smile and says, "She is going to be just fine. Apparently, she was dehydrated due to her, well, umm, extracurricular activities she is engaging in with her friend. Her blood pressure was also a little high, so I put her on a small dose of medicine to manage that and we gave her some IV fluids. I am keeping her overnight, but she's spunky and I have no doubt she'll be back to her routine soon."

Did he just tell me that my grandmother is in the hospital from having too much sex and not hydrating? Oh. My. God.

He nods and leaves us to process all of the information about Grammy.

Harrison gently pulls me to him. I rest my head on his chest, comforted by the sound of his beating heart and his subtle chuckle. He is laughing and I really can't blame him.

I step back and look up at his handsome face. With a straight face, he says, "I suppose Grammy taught us an important lesson about safe sex. Hydration is key." I roll my eyes and head over to Owen, who thankfully didn't hear the whole explanation of her condition. Harrison is still belly laughing.

"Buddy, did you hear that? You're a hero. Your quick thinking saved Grammy's life. I am so grateful for you." He grins at me.

"Does this mean you'll drop Harrison and be my girlfriend?"

I hear Harrison grunt. "Step away from my girl, Owen."

"Can't blame a guy for trying. Addie, I'm hungry. Let's get snacks."

The whole group laughs. At that moment, I wonder if I should be having a discussion of a different type of safe sex with my grandmother.

Harrison

Now that we know Grammy will be fine, I need Jameson to get me that information. The fact that my father, Antonio, and Melanie are all so friendly with each other is troubling. I text Jameson to see if he's free to talk, and my phone rings almost immediately. Sometimes it's as though we share a brain.

"Hey! When are you arriving?" I ask.

"I'll probably be there within the hour. I jumped on the plane as soon as Addie called. How's Nina doing?"

I look over at Nina to find that she's surrounded by her girlfriends. She's lighter now.

"She's shaken, but it helps that Addie and Lillie are here. Mason is on his way, and of course, Owen always makes things better."

Jameson chuckles. "Yes, he does. Listen, I have lots of information about the interconnection of our various parties. Are you ready?"

"No, but I need to get a handle on the situation so that I can help Nina get rid of Antonio and I can be free of my father's ridiculous blackmail scheme."

"Well, it's very interesting. First, Nina didn't get a scholarship from NYU. Your father pulled strings to get her early admission and then paid all of her expenses. Probably just to get her out of town and away from you."

I growl. *He* is the reason she left. Well, I had a part to play in it, but I bet she would have stayed if her college acceptance hadn't been set in stone so early. I could have had the chance to make it right. So much wasted time.

"I found that your father is in some serious debt. Apparently, Lyle loves to gamble. I'm not talking small-time poker. I am talking Vegas-style, private card games where only big money is allowed. That's how he met Antonio. They were at the same card game and your dad lost his ass. Antonio covered him, so then your dad was indebted to Antonio.

"Your father found out about your little affair with Nina in Italy—he probably had people watching you all this time and you never knew it—and wangled a deal. You see, Melanie's father was willing to buy your father's company to pay off his debts and leave him with a nice cushion in exchange for you marrying Melanie, since no other guy of their social status was willing to take her."

I shudder at the thought of a life with Melanie while Jameson continues.

"Your father has kept tabs on Nina all this time. He knew that a year ago, she was looking for a solid investor to help grow her business. He also knew that she would be attending that conference in Vegas. Meanwhile, your father advised Antonio to invest a sizable chunk of money in Nina's business under a fake company name, so she had no idea that either of them was behind it. That was how your father tried to pay back his debt to Antonio. Then your father coordinated Antonio running into Nina and seducing her. They spent the weekend together and through some pre-planned drinking and … other things on Antonio's part, Nina got tricked into a drunken marriage. That was supposed to take her off the market and out of your grasp for good.

"Now, the interesting fact is that Grady has learned from some inside sources that Antonio is bleeding money from some bad investments and bad-luck gambling, and he needs that large investment back from Nina's company. He's in debt to some dangerous people. If he can convince Nina to stay married and make a go of their relationship, then he can get his hands on her money. In case you didn't know, Nina is *quite* successful. She has been pinching pennies for years and has saved an enormous nest egg. You can only imagine what would happen if Antonio stayed in the picture."

I cringe at the thought. Nina has always been a shrewd businesswoman, and I am damn proud of her, more so now than ever before. I refuse to let this two-bit gangster take that away from her.

"Tell me what we need to do," I say.

"Well, you're going to hang tight and support Nina while I get in contact with my FBI buddies. Stay away from Antonio. He's bad news. Desperate men do desperate things. I have the same advice for any interactions with your father. Just make sure that Nina is never alone. I'll take care of everything."

"Thanks, man." My voice shakes with emotion. "Glad you're in my corner." It's amazing how my friends have become family and my family have become strangers. Life has a funny way of showing you the truth.

"I'm working on it from another angle, too. I have a friend who's well-to-do and is always looking for a good investment. Let me talk to him and we'll figure it out together. Don't worry, H. Nina is family, and we have her back."

"Thanks, Jameson. I'll see you soon. I think I'll hold off on telling Nina any of this until we get Grammy back home."

Silence. Then I hear him exhale.

"Don't wait too long. I wouldn't want you repeating my mistakes."

He's got a point. He kept information from Addie while Owen was recovering from being hit by a car, and it almost cost him the love of his life. Still, I don't want Nina to be emotionally destroyed before she finds out the full story about Grammy. She's a strong woman, but everyone has a breaking point, and all of this craziness goes back to the very way she got her start in college. That's painful stuff.

"I won't. We're finally in a good place and I don't want to lose her again. She's *it* for me."

"Damn. I never thought the two of us would fall under the spell of two amazing women, yet here we are."

"If I'm being completely honest, it has always been her. I think I've been in love with her since I was seventeen."

"Look at us. Two grown men talking about their feelings. Shit. We are definitely getting softer every day, but I wouldn't change anything about it."

"Neither would I, which is why we're taking down Antonio and my father. For good."

Nina

All of this seems a bit surreal. After all, earlier today, my Grammy was the poster child of health. Glowing from her bingo speed-dating romp and giggling like a schoolgirl. Happiness looked good on her, and I couldn't help but feel a twinge of envy. She has always been so carefree. No one's opinion of her or us mattered. Her mantra has always been "what other people think of us is not our business." I lost that somewhere along the way.

I notice Harrison's face is hard as he talks to Jameson outside the glass walls that enclose the waiting room. Maddie is asleep on Lillie's lap. Mason just arrived. He sits down next to Lillie and she reaches for his hand. Addie is texting George, letting him know the latest on Grammy. This whole experience makes the reality of her aging so vivid. It's almost as if I think time stands still where she is concerned. While this was a minor incident, it makes me shiver to think about not being so lucky next time. And then there is the reunion. Ugh. What a joke. These ridiculous high school antics seem so trivial now. I allowed years of resentment to eat me alive and it cost me my sanity.

I see a nurse approaching. As I stand, she smiles and ushers me toward the room where my grandmother is resting.

"I know you must be anxious to see her," she whispers.

"I am. Is she awake?" I inquire.

"Yes, and anxious to be released. She's a spitfire. As the doctor told you, we just want to keep her for observation as a precaution."

We enter the dimly lit room. And there in all of her glory is my spunky grandmother.

"When in the hell am I getting out of here?" She scowls.

I lean over the bed rail and kiss her. "Tomorrow. Behave. They just want to hydrate you since your extracurricular activities depleted you." I try to laugh, but the whole situation makes me shudder.

The nurse clears her throat to disguise her chuckle. "If you need anything, I'll be outside at the nurse's station. There's a sofa over here, and I'll bring you a blanket and a pillow. Normally, we don't allow visitors to stay, but I can see that it will benefit both of you, if you do."

"Thank you," I say. Once she leaves, I turn to Grammy and say, "You scared me."

Her eyes soften. "I'm sorry. It scared me too."

Grateful I can stay with her, I pull over the nearby chair and settle in next to the bed. We spend the next hour revisiting our life together. Reminiscing about the past and making amends over not coming home enough. Regret. I have so much of it. I have built this emotional wall around me. I thought it would protect me, but the reality is nothing protects anyone from hurt. Loving people is an honor, and I can't keep avoiding it. It's making me hollow.

"Hey. How is she doing?" Mason's voice jolts me out of my slumber. Apparently we had both fallen asleep while walking down my own memory lane.

"Annoyed that she's here. Scared that it happened, but grateful she can go home tomorrow."

"I could have gone my whole life not knowing the circumstances that led her here." He grimaces.

"Enough about her sex life. I want to hear something that doesn't make my ears bleed. I've been dying to know what's happening with you and Lillie."

Mason blushes and turns away from me. My spirit lifts; I have *never* seen him react to a woman this way.

"She is a very nice person, and we enjoy each other's company."

"I can tell that I'm not going to get the dirt from you. No worries, I'll interrogate Lillie," I tease.

"Nina, please don't. This is so hard for me. You know emotions are difficult with my autism. Let me just say that Lillie and Maddie are special. I like being with them. I understand Maddie and what she's experiencing, so it makes me feel like I belong."

Tears stream down my face as I grab Mason's hands. Normally, he's not a fan of touch, but he seems receptive, and I bet Lillie is the reason.

"You have always belonged. You're one of my people, Mason, and I'm grateful for you. Don't ever think you don't fit in—you do. I love you."

He squeezes my hand and gives me a small smile. That's a big deal for him. In the past, he would have abruptly left the room due to his discomfort. He's different. I may have to suggest Lillie work remotely and move here permanently. Hell, maybe I'll make the move too. What the hell is happening to me?

Nina

I inhale Harrison's scent and nestle closer to his chest. Why have I been so stubborn? Denying this attraction. Feeling the security of having someone in my corner is an enormous relief. Why have I been so resistant?

"You had every reason to distrust me, Nina."

Oh shit. I must have shared my thoughts out loud. Just another indication that I've been around Addie way too much. I'm becoming filterless.

"Sorry. I was just thinking and didn't mean to vocalize my thoughts." I back away and shrug, not meeting his eyes.

He gently lifts my chin so our eyes meet. "Nina, there have been so many obstacles to us being together, but we are very much a unit. You are mine and I am yours. We just need to focus on Grams and eliminating my father and Antonio from the picture."

I chuckle. "You make it sound like we're in a mob movie. Are we putting concrete blocks around their feet and dropping them into the river?"

Harrison is deadly quiet, and his face becomes like stone. Wow, he gets hotter when he's angry.

"What's wrong? You're kind of scaring me and turning me on at the same time."

He smirks. "Well, let's come back to the turning you on part later, but for now, there's some information about Antonio and my father that you need to know."

"Okay. Care to share?"

Before he can utter a word, Grammy's doctor steps into view. Harrison squeezes my hand.

"How is she doing?" I ask.

"Her vitals are good. When she woke up briefly, she was alert and in good spirits. I'm planning on releasing her in the morning with her new medication, along with instructions to take it easy for a couple of days." He smirks and I shake my head.

"Okay. Thank you so much. The taking-it-easy part might be a challenge, but there are enough of us to keep her down for a few days at least."

"Go home and get some rest. I do rounds early, so she'll be discharged well before noon tomorrow."

"Sounds good. I appreciate all your help." I smile. He nods and walks down the corridor.

"Let me take you home so you can get some rest."

"No, I want to stay with her. This whole situation scared me and I would feel better saying with her."

"I can stay too if you want company." He rubs my back, which feel amazing, by the way.

"Go on and go home. No reason both of us are exhausted tomorrow."

"Alright. I am only agreeing because I don't want to argue with you. Want to walk me out?"

"Absolutely." I grin.

Addie

I see them before they see me. Harrison and Nina are walking together, their hands intertwined and Nina looking at peace. Sweet. Baby. Jesus. I have been waiting for this moment for what seems like forever. While I'm mooning over the scene, arms wrap around my waist and a deep voice whispers softly in my ear.

"Are you spying on our friends?"

A grin spreads across my face and I abruptly turn around to greet Jameson's handsome face.

"Of course I am. Look at them. They are fucking adorable. Finally! It feels like it took so long." I'm a little giddy. Kind of like a small child at Christmas. "By the way, I'm very happy to see you."

"How happy?" He winks.

"Happy enough to give you a little PDA." I smooch him with no regrets.

"Are we interrupting?" Nina inquires.

I turn around and do a little happy dance. Nina shakes her head at me and laughs. "What are you doing?"

"I'm doing a happy dance because I saw you holding hands. Are you two finally together?"

"I guess so. I mean, you know, until something better comes along." She shrugs and slyly grins.

Harrison grabs her face and crashes his lips to hers. He releases her, appearing quite smug, and she looks dazed.

"So yeah, we are definitely together and nothing better will come along." She laughs.

"How's Grammy?" I reach for her hand and squeeze it.

"She's good. The doctor says she can go home tomorrow, but she needs to take it easy."

I snort. I haven't known Nina's grandmother very long, but she will be a challenge to keep still.

"No snorting necessary. I know that it will be a difficult, but I have lots of help."

"Of course, we'll all help. Just tell us what we can do." I beg to help because this woman—my very best friend—has walked through the fires of hell with me. I would do anything for her. If she murdered someone, I would help her bury the body. If she committed a crime, I would hide her away. Well, you get the gist. I'm not aiming to aid and abet, but I would do it for her.

"I think it would be best if we all got some rest. We can regroup in the morning."

"Sounds good. We can bring some breakfast over in the morning and help with anything else you need."

"Addie, I need to chat with them before I head back to the room," Jameson says. "Do you want me to bring you a hot chocolate and a donut with sprinkles?"

It's hot when a former Navy SEAL says a dainty word like "sprinkles."

"Yes, please, and I hope that you'll fill me in because you know how I despise being out of the loop." I pout.

Jameson kisses my forehead and says, "I'll tell you everything. I learned that lesson the hard way."

I grin at him and wave them off as I head back to the B&B, while the three of them unravel the mystery of Nina's life.

Nina

We head to the parking lot in silence. My anxiety level is through the roof. The quiet is cut by a bellowing, screeching voice that only can belong to one person. Melanie.

"Harrison! Wait! I have something I need to tell you. It's important."

We all stop and turn toward the direction of the voice. I feel Harrison's hand stiffen in mine.

"Stalking us now?" I sneer.

She cocks her hip and narrows her beady, little eyes. "This is a private conversation between my fiancé and me."

"I am not your fiancé, Melanie, so just state your business. There is *nothing* you can say that Jameson and Nina can't be present for. In fact, I insist on it, as I need witnesses to whatever craziness you're about to spout."

"Fine. I'm pregnant."

I stand there frozen. What. The. Actual. Fuck. Pregnant? Then I start to laugh uncontrollably. Tears running down my face. The type of laughter that barely provides a breath. Now I look like the crazy one.

"Poor Melanie. You do know that you actually have to have sex with the person in order for conception to happen. Wait. That's right. You weren't always terribly bright." I smirk.

Harrison remains quiet. Too quiet.

"Harrison, do you have anything to say about this?"

"Melanie, how do you know it's mine?"

Woah. What? Oh. My. God. It's happening again. I open myself up and I am betrayed.

"What are you talking about Harrison? You haven't been with her since high school, right?"

He turns to me and says, "After Italy, I was so upset about us not moving forward that I went to a bar and got wasted. I was on my way out to grab a cab home when I ran into Melanie. But I don't remember anything else. I ended up at her apartment, but I'm pretty sure I passed out. I can't remember if anything happened, I just know she's lying. I know it."

My heart drops. "So you were upset about us, got drunk, and proceeded to impregnate Melanie? You don't think you had sex. Seriously? Once a manwhore, always a manwhore. I hope you both have an amazing life. You deserve each other. I will leave you to work out your mess while I go sit with my grandmother. There is such a stench in this parking lot that I must go get some fresh air."

Jameson, a man of few words, nods at me and then glares at Harrison, who is pulling at his hair. He looks like he wants to punch someone.

"Nina, wait. Don't leave," he begs.

"I can't keep doing this with you."

I turn and walk away while Harrison starts screaming at Melanie and she begins to cry. What a shitshow.

Harrison

I've lost count of how many times I have watched her walk away, and each time it falls on me. My fault. My heart clenches. I turn back to Melanie, who has stopped crying and now wears a grin.

"Tell me the truth. Whose baby is it, because I know you haven't been celibate."

"Harrison, I swear. It's ours. I have only ever wanted you." She tries to grab my hand, but I swat her away.

"I need proof. I don't trust you. If it is mine, I'll care for the child, but we are *nothing*. The only woman I love is Nina. It has always been Nina."

Her face contorts and she hisses, "Nina isn't good enough for you and besides, she's already married. This baby needs both of its parents and you will do right by me. Our fathers will see to it."

"Are you threatening me?"

"All I'm saying is that you would be smart to do what was originally planned, that way nothing will happen to Nina. If you love her, then do the right thing."

"The right thing is to spend the rest of my life with Nina. But don't worry, Melanie, once I prove you're lying, you and our families can go fuck yourselves."

"Is that any way to talk to the mother of your child?" she gasps.

"That has yet to be determined."

I walk away from her and get into my car. I know seeing Nina right now is not an option, so I call Jameson. He's going to kick my ass.

"What the fuck did you do?" I can tell he's gritting his teeth as he speaks.

I ignore the question.

"How is she?" I whisper.

"She's devastated, pissed, heartbroken, and well, the list goes on. What were you thinking?"

"I wasn't. Honestly, I don't remember much about that night. I had a lot to drink and then Melanie showed up. After that, I couldn't tell you what happened. I can't do anything but get the proof that she's lying about being pregnant with my child. I was so drunk that there was no way I could perform."

"Harrison, it's not just the pregnancy. It's the fact that you were with someone not long after you and Nina were together in Italy. Now, I get that you were upset, but put yourself in her position. How would you feel if the roles were reversed?"

I ponder that. I would feel like shit. I would want to punch the douche who touched her. It's more than jealousy. It's like she's a part of me.

"I really fucked up."

Jameson exhales. "Yeah, you did, but the good news is that we can work to prove that Melanie is lying. The bad news is that you have to convince Nina you've changed, and judging by your recent transgression, that might be difficult. Oh, and Addie is going to castrate you."

Jesus. I am in so much trouble.

Nina

Early the next morning, there's a knock on the hospital door. I am not pleased to find Harrison along with Jameson on the threshold, but I'm hoping they at least have some answers. I am exhausted from all the antics. My life sounds like a badly made movie with incredibly incompetent actors. I'm only interested in answers at this point. Somehow. Some way. I need my life back. I step into the hallway, close the door, and motion to a small waiting area in an effort not to disturb Grammy.

"How is she?" Harrison asks.

"She's sleeping but is doing well. Hopefully we will be out of here in a few hours." I tap my foot impatiently.

The guys exchange a look, and Harrison proceeds.

"First of all, I'm going prove I didn't sleep with Melanie and that everything she said is a lie."

I start to interrupt him because I certainly am done with his manwhoring ways, but he holds up his hand, which really pisses me off.

"Second, all of this was set in motion by my father."

I nod, not really surprised.

"This isn't going to be easy to hear, but just listen until the end. My father set up your NYU early admittance and paid your way through school in an effort to get you away from me. Apparently, he thought that by removing you, I would be more compliant to his whims. When he successfully removed you from the equation, he thought he would be able to control me, but he didn't count on my grandfather leaving me half his estate, which practically crippled my parents financially. You see, my father did well with his business, but he and my mother spend well over what they make, and without my grandfather's full inheritance, they were circling the drain. He still had someone keeping tabs on me, so when he heard that we were together in Italy, he found a way to pounce."

"How does Antonio fit into all of this?" I ask.

"My father got in deeper with his gambling, which he had hoped would offset his financial issues. He was in a high-stakes poker game where he lost his ass, but Antonio covered him in exchange for a favor. He was looking for a reputable company to invest in so he could appear legit. My father suggested your company since he knew you were looking for silent investors."

"What. The. Actual. Fuck. How did he know that?" I spat.

"We don't know, but he set it up and then coordinated your chance meeting with Antonio while you were in Vegas for the conference."

My head is spinning with this information. I can't even process that my life has been a series of orchestrated events. It's like I was simply a chess piece in someone else's game.

They look at each other. Jameson nods at Harrison. He takes a big breath and exhales.

"We believe you may have been roofied. You told Addie that you only had two drinks. That doesn't warrant you being blind drunk." Harrison grabs my hand and squeezes.

"*What?!*" I holler. I can't believe what I'm hearing.

"We don't have proof of it, but it would make sense since you remember nothing after dinner the last night you were there."

I am silenced with that layer of information as he continues.

"Two days later, you had a new investor. I remember how excited you were. The transaction was through his lawyer and there was no reason to suspect anything. It seemed on the up-and-up. Which, by the way, it is. He hasn't done anything illegal using your company. His investment is just a front to make him look legit. He's small-time and looking to grow. With that being said, he can't lose you. He's losing ground after making enemies with some not so nice people. He needs your agency and the money that comes with it."

I open my mouth to speak, but nothing comes out. This is just so much to take in. I try again, and this time my voice comes out. "So I'm in danger, right? And so is everyone I love."

"We won't let anything happen to you. Jameson already reported everything he knows to his FBI buddies, and they're working on a sting to bring Antonio down. We need access to your financials to turn over to them."

"No problem. I'll have Lillie get that together and send them to you. What about your father?" I hate this for Harrison. I mean, he never had a great relationship with the bastard, but to learn just how diabolical the man is must be heart-wrenching.

"We have enough evidence to bring him down. Let's just say Bitsy might have to get a job at the country club."

I laugh at that image. It's just the release I need.

Harrison looks at Jameson and clears his throat. "Unfortunately, both my father and Antonio have disappeared, so we have bodyguards in place for your protection. Don't worry, that includes Grammy and everyone in your circle."

Not going to lie, I'm a wee bit scared, but for whatever reason, a giggle escapes, and I look at the two ridiculously handsome men in my house and say, "Addie is going to have a field day with this. Please tell me that this situation doesn't rival hers. I want her to win in the shitshow department."

They chuckle and Jameson says, "She knows there's no competition. She wins hands down."

"Nina, I know you're angry with me, but I will do everything in my power to regain your trust."

I don't know if that's even possible.

Nina

As I head back to the room after that disconcerting conversation, I am accosted by George, who flew in once he heard about Grammy. I am so lucky to have such amazing friends. George grabs me in an overdramatic hug.

"I hope your grammy will be okay. I'm so upset for her and for you," he says.

"George, you really didn't need to come. She is going to be fine," I say. "However, selfishly, I am glad you're here. I can't believe all of the craziness that has happened over the past few days."

"Girl, you and Addie have more drama in your life than I can keep up with, but I'm glad you're safe, and I do enjoy when your men hire bodyguards." He wiggles his eyebrows.

Sure enough, the agency Jameson contacted has put their men in place. They are strategically placed in front of Grammy's hospital room. Oh, and there is one trailing me too. They work fast. Apparently, this is Harrison's way of always being around, which is super awkward to say the least. Nothing brings people together like a crazed, mobster husband and an equally delusional father.

"George, I hope they're up to your specifications." I giggle.

"Oh honey. Jameson always picks out the hottest ones. Perfect eye candy for Grammy and her recovery."

I squeeze George's hand and reach to open the door. The nurse has ignored how many people keep rotating in and out of her room. Addie pops up as she sees us enter and embraces George.

Grammy is dressed and ready to go. "It's about time you got here. I am so ready to go home." Patience is not her virtue. "I have a feeling you have some things to tell me since we seem to have some new additions to the group." She eyes the bodyguards.

"There have been some developments and I will fill you in once we get home."

"I need to ask the doctor if there are any restrictions, if you know what I mean." She winks at me.

"Unfortunately, I do, and I would prefer not to," I hiss.

She grins at me as the doctor walks in with her final instructions. I, like the mature woman that I am, plug my ears while George and Addie giggle like two schoolchildren. The nurse brings the discharge papers and George helps Grammy into the wheelchair while she complains that she can walk just fine.

I take the papers and prescription for her high blood pressure medicine along with her purse and follow our entourage that now includes bodyguards. Welcome to my life.

Nina

I exhale as we walk into Grammy's home. The smell of food permeates the air. Her bingo friends made sure she wouldn't be slaving over a hot stove for a while. So grateful she has a good support system.

"Ready to take a nap?" I ask, hoping that I can put off our little discussion about my interesting life.

"Not until you tell me about the bodyguards. What the hell happened since I've been in the hospital?"

"Don't get upset. It's not good for your blood pressure."

"I won't be upset if you simply tell me what is going on, Nina."

I spill it all. It's a like a tsunami as I vomit all the bizarre information that describes what is happening in my life.

"I am currently married, and my spouse is operating on a criminal level, and oh, my boyfriend's father has it out for me. The icing on the cake is that Harrison got Melanie pregnant. Although he denies it. This is currently my life."

She remains silent. I hold my breath. The last thing I want to do is cause her more distress than she is already experiencing.

"That is certainly a whole lot of drama. You must be exhausted between that and dealing with my little hospital excursion. I do know this. Harrison loves you. He always has, so you need to trust that. Melanie is a troublemaker. Always has been. I have always told you to assume positive intent when it comes to the people you love. Give that to Harrison until you have more information."

I ponder what she has said, and I hate to admit that she's right. Melanie has not been known to be truthful in the past, and Harrison looked devasted when I simply dismissed him.

"You're right. I was so consumed with hearing that he actually left with Melanie from a bar not too long after Italy, that I simply stopped listening to him. Grammy. I seem to always be looking for an exit as an excuse not to deal with my feelings."

"Sweetie, you have got to open yourself up. No one can avoid hurt. If you don't open your heart, you are going to miss out on something magical. Now, I'm going upstairs to take a nap. Are you going to be okay?"

"Yes. I have a lot to think about, but I think I'll take a nap too. Maybe my head will be clearer with some rest."

"Sounds like a great idea. I'm always here for you. I love you, sweet girl." She hugs me and I can't help but get teary. She is my rock.

"I love you too, Grammy. Get some rest and then we can eat some of the amazing food your friends brought."

She heads upstairs as I shed my shoes and plop on the couch. My eyes become heavy immediately. Just a few minutes to rest, then I'll get in the shower. You know the delightful space between light and heavy sleep where you feel like you're floating? I'm there until I feel like someone is staring at me. I open my eyes. My body jolts.

Antonio.

"How did you get in here?" I gasp.

He cocks his head. "Did you really think a couple of bodyguards would stop me?"

My blood runs cold.

"Don't worry, sweetheart. I only knocked them out with tranquilizers. I'm a lover, not a killer. Blood makes me squeamish."

"Seriously? Antonio, aren't you supposed to be a mobster?" I am baffled at his admission.

"Mobster is such an ugly term. I prefer businessman with questionable ethics." He chuckles at his own attempt at a joke. I am not amused.

"What do you want?" Suddenly I'm not afraid. I mean, he isn't doing a great job of intimidating me. I just need to keep him talking. My phone was next to me, but when I sat down, it slid under one of the pillows. Antonio starts pacing the room, not paying one bit of attention to me. He's rambling on and on about God only knows what—I can barely hear him, I'm so nervous—so I take the opportunity to grab my phone. I glance down and tap Harrison's name on my favorites. It rings and I'm praying he answers. Meanwhile, Antonio starts talking about our marriage and how he needs me, so we need to make it official. I hear Harrison answer and I immediately put it on speaker.

"What do you mean, Antonio?"

"Oh, well, I had the marriage certificate forged. It made things easier since you were so out of it. Now we just have to make it official."

Delusional much?

"That isn't going to happen, Antonio. You've committed a laundry list of crimes. I don't have any experience, but I'm pretty sure that the foundation for a happy union isn't one that you're forced into joining."

"You will learn to love me. Your business is helping me appear legit. I'm slowly gaining respect from the other Vegas bosses. I just need to keep up appearances. If they find out about my losses … That just can't happen."

His distorted perception might be even more dangerous, especially when he pulls out a vial that I can only assume would be a tranquilizer of some sort. I mean, a nap would be great, but I prefer to do that on my own terms. He fills the syringe and walks toward me with a glint in his eyes. All I can think of is Grammy and the fact that she's upstairs without protection.

"Don't worry, my love. The next time you wake up, you'll be safely tucked away in Vegas, where we'll be officially married."

As he approaches me, I see Grammy out of the corner of my eye. She is scowling and carrying a lamp. I watch the scene unfold as if I were having an out-of-body experience. Antonio approaches me with the syringe, and the front door opens behind him. He turns at the sound and notices Grammy as she swings the lamp at him, but before he can react, she slams it against his head, shattering the base, and he falls to the ground like a sack of potatoes.

"Asshole!" she screams as he lies on the ground.

I am so stunned at my badass grandmother standing over Antonio, I almost miss the dramatic entrance of Harrison, Jameson, and some official-looking men.

Harrison rushes to my side as the officials remove Antonio from the room.

"Are you okay? Jesus, Nina, you scared the shit out of me."

To be honest, I wasn't sure how this was going to end, but I knew that my destiny was never to be a mafia princess.

"I'm fine. Who knew that my grandmother was a superhero?"

Grammy sits down next to me and grabs my hand. "I heard him while I was in my bedroom. He certainly wasn't quiet with his confession, so I snuck down and did what I had to do. Nobody is going to hurt my baby."

"You could have been hurt. Why didn't you just call 911?" There is a harsh tone in my voice as I realize this could have gone a different way.

"I just reacted. I knew that if I called 911, they wouldn't be able to get here in time, and I didn't want him to hurt you." Her eyes glisten with tears.

"I had called Harrison without Antonio knowing, so he could hear what was happening. I thought I had things under control if I could keep him talking, but he was bound and determined to sedate me and take me back to Vegas." I shudder at the thought.

"I knew I raised a smart cookie." She leans over to hug me, and I inhale her goodness. I am so lucky to have her in my life. The moment is interrupted by a booming voice.

"You both scared the shit out me," Harrison says.

"It's not like we planned this, so stop scowling. Both of us are fine. You did hear him admit that the marriage certificate was forged, right? I'm a free woman."

"We'll see about that," he says.

Before I can respond, we're interrupted by an agent who wants to ask me some questions. The things I have to say to Harrison can wait. After all, what's a few more hours?

Harrison

Understandably, when you get a phone call from the person you love and they're in immediate danger, you might overreact. Fortunately, Jameson is with me, and he helps me maintain my calm. There are already FBI agents in town following Antonio, but they were given the slip. Once Jameson informs them of the location, all hell breaks loose and we head straight to Grammy's house at top speed.

"Now when we get there, let these guys take the lead. We don't know what state Antonio is in, and we certainly don't want Nina hurt if you bulldoze your way in there."

I glare at him and rub my hand down my face. "I hear you, but if this were Addie …" I stop talking because he knows what he's talking about. He was a Navy SEAL, after all.

"Look, man, trust me when I say that emotions never serve a purpose in a rescue mission. Nina is smart. She figured out a way to call you, and because of her, Antonio is going down. I get it. Nina is part of our tribe. Addie will have my balls if anything happens to her."

I laugh because Addie has his balls anyway.

We pull up to the house to find the agents swarming out of their vehicle and up to the door, surprisingly quiet for their number and speed. They quickly remove the unconscious bodyguards from the doorway and get in position. Once the door opens, it's organized chaos. What I witness next is like a live-action movie. Antonio with a syringe. Nina, eyes wide. Grammy hitting Antonio over the head with a lamp. His look of surprise followed by his body crumbling to the ground. Holy hell, Grammy is a ninja.

Nina

After the house is cleared of Antonio and hot agents, I'm eager to shower and change my clothes. Finally. Jesus, this has been the longest day ever. Jameson and Harrison headed back to the hotel. Apparently, they have some information on the infamous, asshole father. I could tell Harrison wanted to stay, but I am so glad he left. I just want to be alone for a short time to process all of this. Addie is going to be here any minute, and I know I won't get any peace after that. She's like a tornado. A sweet, loving, hilarious tornado. Speak of the devil.

The door bursts open and she arrives in all of her glory. Her face is fierce as she hurls herself forward and grabs me in a tight hug. She puts in extra squeezes for good measure.

"Are you alright? Do you need a doctor? What the fuck happened? Is it true Grammy took down the big mobster with a lamp? Damn, girl. She's a badass."

"Breathe, Addie. I'm fine. Antonio was all talk and no action. Well, he was almost action, but Grammy saved me." I wave my hand, dismissing the notion that I might have been a tiny bit terrified.

"Well holy hotness, did you see the band of merry men that came to rescue you? I thought George was going to have a stroke when they all gathered at the B&B. Of course, Jameson is the hottest, but you should have seen Harrison. I thought he was going rip someone apart. Oh, and did he tell you about his dad?" Her eyes twinkle with delight.

"I did notice the intensely hot group of testosterone that stormed in to rescue me, but only afterward because I was a bit busy trying not to be kidnapped and forced to be a mafia princess."

"Of course! You would be a horrible mafia princess because you're kind of bossy, and I think they like their women a bit submissive. Anyway, about Lyle—"

"I don't want to talk about any of that right now. My body is sizzling from all the adrenaline, and I just want to take a breath. I sent Grammy to back to her room to lie down. I'm sure her blood pressure is ridiculously high, and I don't want her to stroke out on me."

"Look, I really think you should talk to Harrison. I think there's more to the story and I'm sure Melanie is lying. She is such a bitch."

"It doesn't matter. He jumped in bed with my worst nightmare after I told him we couldn't be together, *right* after we'd slept together. I can't be with someone like that." I shrug.

"You told him you couldn't be with him. He was single. I hate to point out the obvious, but you let him go. He was free to do what he wanted. I know that is a harsh reality. He didn't cheat on you, so why are you punishing him?"

I despise when wise Addie shows up. She's right, but I can't let go of the fact that he slept with and produced a baby with Melanie.

"I am not punishing him." I sound like a petulant toddler.

"You are an emotional runner. This is your pattern. Your walls are always up. I get it. Love is a risk and sometimes you get hurt, but if you don't open yourself up, you miss out on all the good stuff that comes with it. Do you want to be alone forever?"

I contemplate what she just shared. There is validity in her statement. I run to avoid feelings. I put up walls to avoid attachments. My trust issues are deep. I look at my friend who has overcome her own struggles with abandonment and trust. She is the perfect representation of stepping out of her comfort zone and seizing love.

"Addie, you are so right. I avoid. I run. I am terrified, and when Melanie showed up with her announcement, I didn't wait for Harrison to explain. Everything is such a mess right now." I'm practically shouting with my own epiphany.

"Well, then you need to figure out how you want your story to play out, my friend. The ball is in your court." She pauses. "And it seems you didn't get a chance to shower yet." She scrunches her nose at me as if I smell like garbage. I sniff my pits because refined Nina is not the same as Addie's-best-friend Nina.

"No, I was very busy trying not to be kidnapped, but I will right now." I stand up and move toward the stairs.

"When you're done, I'll tell you the story of Lyle and his penchant for lingerie." She cackles.

I pause on the steps. Why would Lyle's infidelity be such a big deal? I shrug and say, "Okay. I'll be right back." I can still hear her laughing. I wonder what the joke is.

Nina

Feeling refreshed and obviously smelling better, I head back downstairs to hear the riveting story that Addie is chomping at the bit to share. My steps falter as I run into a hard chest halfway to the first floor. I know that chest.

"I didn't think you would be coming back. Don't you have to attend to your baby mama?" I sneer. Apparently, my epiphany left the building, and I am still bitchy.

"I have news about my father that I thought you should hear." He tries to sound unaffected by my harsh words, but I can see the hurt in his eyes.

"Oh, Addie did say something about him loving lingerie, so I assumed that he was cheating on your mom. Who is the unfortunate soul who's getting it on with your dad?"

"Please never say 'getting it on' again when referencing my father." He shudders and I can't help but giggle.

"Come on. Let's eat. I brought burgers from the diner. Jameson and Addie are waiting for us. Addie just checked on Grammy, and she is sleeping. Apparently, being a superhero is exhausting."

We walk into the kitchen where they are already seating with our plates filled with food. I didn't realize how hungry I am until the aroma tickles my nose. My stomach growls. Addie laughs at me and says, "I bet your stomach doesn't make any noise when you eat that kale crap."

She's right, but I won't admit that to her. Tonight, I will indulge in this juicy burger and greasy fries. The best comfort food for after you've been almost tranquilized and kidnapped.

I sit down in between Harrison and Addie, with Jameson across from me. With the first bite of my burger, I'm in heaven.

"If you don't tell her the dirt, I will, Harrison. I can't wait to see her face."

He sighs. "It appears that my dad enjoys wearing women's lingerie."

"Oh, well, okay. Each to their own." I shrug and continue to eat my burger.

Addie raises her eyebrow at him, and he closes his eyes while shaking his head.

"That's not the only thing. Apparently, he's a drag queen."

I stop chewing and turn my head to face him. Bless his heart. Harrison is horrified, and I'm trying not to laugh. I mean, there's nothing funny about drag queens. Their self-expression is absolutely enviable—I wish I had that much confidence. But the thought that Lyle McCall—the most pretentious ass on the planet, the man who relishes his masculine appearance—is a drag queen is beyond hysterical. I must keep my composure. However, I make the mistake of looking at Addie. Her eyes are big as saucers and her face is red from keeping in the laughter. She starts giggling and then the whole table erupts in fits of hysterics. Well, everyone except Harrison. He is clearly uncomfortable. I reach over and squeeze his hand, but quickly remove it.

"I'm so sorry for laughing. It's just that the image of Lyle McCall on a stage dressed in women's clothing is just too much for my brain to handle. I am being insensitive to you. Tell me what else you learned."

I go back to eating my burger as a way to distract myself, but also because I am starving.

"Well, my father cooked his books and evaded paying taxes, so there's now a warrant for his arrest. You can imagine that my mother is beside herself and is trying to find solace in a bottle of gin. Their assets have been frozen—whatever might be left."

Woah. How the mighty have fallen.

"I'm sorry you had to learn all that awful stuff about your father," I say. "We all knew he was a jerk, but wow, that's a new level. This has been a really crazy day."

We clean up the kitchen. Jameson and Harrison head to the front door, but Addie stays behind and turns toward me.

"Nina, you look exhausted. Go get some sleep. You need all your energy for your reunion tomorrow," Addie quips.

I groan. "I am not going, and you know why."

"Yes, you are. Now, Jameson and I are going to go back to the B&B. Lillie was kind enough to hang out with Owen, so I'm sure he has been forcing her to do dance videos with him. She is probably ready to pass out from exhaustion."

"You can't make me go," I state.

"Challenge accepted. Besides, Cassie and Marley can't wait. They want to see your former classmates' reactions. After all, you are this successful literary agent who lives in NYC. You are stunning. It's going to be epic. Speaking of, can you please call your friends? They're worried about you. I assured them you were fine, but I think they would like to hear it from you. Oh, and talk to Harrison. You'll regret it if you don't."

She squeezes my arm and we walk to the front door to join the guys.

"Harrison, do you think we could talk tomorrow?" I ask.

I can barely believe I gathered the courage to say that because old Nina simply walks away, but he deserves to share his side of the story.

"Absolutely. Do you want to go to breakfast?"

I can see the hope in his eyes.

"Sure. Let's meet at the diner at eight o'clock."

"Sounds good. Thank you for being willing to listen. I'll see you in the morning. Get some rest. The bodyguards are still out front since Lyle is on the loose."

"Okay. Goodnight you guys, and thanks for everything."

I shut the door behind them and sigh.

Harrison

I nervously await Nina's arrival. Sleep was evasive and honestly, I have no idea what I'm going to say. I'm just grateful she's willing to sit down and hear what I have to say. I see her before she sees me. God, she is beautiful. Even with everything she has gone through, she radiates beauty. Inside and outside. She turns and our eyes meet. I smile and she walks toward the table. I bounce out of my seat and pull out the chair for her. See? Chivalry is not dead. I sit back down, and silence blankets the table. Before, I can utter a word, the waitress stops by asking for our drink orders. Both of us request coffee.

"Did you sleep okay?" I inquire.

"Yes. Apparently, attempted kidnapping is exhausting," she quips.

"That was scary, Nina. Don't make light of it. Thinking of you and Grammy in danger, well, I can't even think about it without getting angry. You both could have been seriously hurt." My words are harsh but true. The scenario could have turned out completely different.

"But it worked out and we're fine. Grammy slept well and she's eating breakfast with Mason, Lillie, and sweet Maddie."

"What's the story there?"

"Not sure. I think it may be a love match, but they're keeping things quiet. It's the first time Mason has been this comfortable around a woman. I fear I may lose my assistant."

The waitress brings our coffee and we order breakfast. As she leaves, we resume our conversation.

"I want to tell you about that night when Melanie claims we slept together."

"Okay. Go ahead. I want to hear your side of the story."

I take a deep breath.

"I was devastated that you didn't want to take a chance on us, so I went to a bar to drink away my sorrow. I thought after Italy, we would be together and I couldn't believe you just dismissed that possibility. I was hurt. After a few drinks, I decided to call a car and go home, but before I could do that, I ran into Melanie. She told me she was visiting a friend and honestly, I hadn't seen her in forever. We chatted and she persuaded me to have a drink with her."

Nina closes her eyes and shakes her head. I continue.

"I didn't think I was that drunk, but the bourbon was smooth and I probably overdid it. She kissed me. I do remember that, and I kissed her back." I stop. Nina's eyes are open and wet with tears. I want to touch her. I take a breath and proceed with the rest of the story.

"After I kissed her, I looked at her in horror. I couldn't believe I'd done that. There was no excuse for it. She wasn't you. Melanie was understanding when I told her the kiss was a mistake. I should have seen that as a red flag. Melanie has never been one to put anyone else's feelings first. She insisted on getting me a car and making sure I got home okay. I told her that wasn't necessary, but honestly, I was completely shitfaced and my faculties were all fucked up. We got to my apartment and then I passed out in my bed. When I woke up the next morning, Melanie was asleep next to me. I froze and tried to piece together the night. Nina, I swear nothing happened."

Silence thickens between us. The waitress brings our food, which is unappetizing at this point, but we use it as a distraction. Both of us take bites as Nina processes what I just shared.

"How do you know you didn't sleep with her if you were so drunk?" Her eyes are still focused on her food. She won't even look at me.

"All I can tell you is that I know. I already told Melanie that she would need to have a paternity test, but hell, I don't even believe she's pregnant."

"I just don't know what to believe. I feel like I'm simply a pawn in a chess game. Harrison, I can't move forward until this mess is cleaned up. That means I can't be with you. Too much has happened, and I need some time. I really have no reason to be mad. After all, I did tell you we couldn't be in a relationship, but for some reason, it really bothers me."

"Nina, you have feelings for me. Just like I have feelings for you. Of course, this is going to bother you. If the roles were reversed, I would want to kick the guy's ass. I will do whatever it takes to make this right. I promise."

Her eyes meet mine.

"You know I have trust issues, and like I said, it shouldn't matter since we were not together, but it does. Let's take some time. We need to get through the wedding and then we can regroup."

"I can work with that. Are you okay after everything that happened yesterday? How is Grammy?" I take a breath and relax a little.

"I'm okay. Really, I am and so is Grammy. She's anxious to get back out there and live her life, but she agreed to giving herself one more day of rest since yesterday was really fucked up." She chuckles and shakes her head.

"Yesterday took about ten years off my life. I'm just glad you both are okay."

We continue to eat and make small talk. The reunion is tonight, and I'm going to make sure that I have the proof I need to confirm that Melanie is lying. Jameson is working on a lead and I'm hoping to have that by tonight. Nina is not getting away from me this time.

Nina

B reakfast was a mindfuck. I am in love with that man. This I know, but with everything that has happened, I really just want to be alone and decompress. Sounds lovely, right? Well, apparently I can't have that, because Marley, Cassie, and Addie are blowing up my phone about the reunion. Ugh. I am not in the mindset to go. Really. I just want to hang out at Grammy's, eat junk food, and wallow. Unfortunately, peer pressure still exists even after high school.

I decide to go to the park that I used to go to when I needed a place to think growing up. Nestled under a tree is my favorite bench. I spent a lot of time here. A smile spreads across my face when I see Mason reading on a bench nearby.

I walk over and sit next to him.

"Hey! I haven't seen you in a while. How are you?"

"I'm fine, but you are the one who has been through a lot. Are you okay?"

"Yes. No. I have no idea. My relationship with Harrison is weird. Melanie is supposedly pregnant with his baby. I now know I'm not really married. Harrison's dad is MIA and the ringleader for fucking up my life. I just don't know."

We sit in quiet contemplation. Mason isn't one to dole out advice, which is why he's good to vent to. He listens intently and sometimes comes through with some profound thought. I'm hoping that's what will happen now.

"Humans are fallible. Mistakes happen. Only looking at someone's fault doesn't let you really see them." He shrugs, staring at the children playing on the playground.

And, my friends, Mason delivered exactly what I needed, though I still need some time to process everything. At least I can start looking at the goodness that Harrison brings. God knows I'm not perfect, so why do I feel I have license to judge? My past does not dictate my future, and I have been a prisoner too long. It's time to move forward.

"Wow! Mason, that was so wise. I needed to hear that, so thank you. Want to share what's going on with you and Lillie?" I nudge him with my shoulder.

"She is nice, and I enjoy her company. Plus, I think I help Maddie. I can relate to her, and I'm learning sign language so we can communicate." He gives a slight smile. A rare occurrence in my experience.

"I'm happy for you, Mason. You deserve only the very best, and Lillie is amazing. I knew when I hired her that she was something special. What's going to happen when she goes back to New York in a few days?"

"I don't know. I might move there. My job can be done remotely, and I don't want to be alone anymore."

I grab his hand. He doesn't resist my touch. Lillie and Maddie have done the impossible. I have never seen Mason so content and at peace. His social anxiety seems to have calmed, and it's all due to those sweet humans.

"Well, I for one would love to have you in New York. This is a big step. I am so proud of you." Tears stream down my face.

"This is all new and strange for me, but it feels right."

At least one of us knows how to move forward. I just hope I can figure out what I need to do.

Harrison

With Jameson's help, we have proof that Melanie is indeed lying. Well, she is pregnant, but I'm not the baby daddy. I know you want an explanation, and trust me, you will be surprised, but I need to tell Nina first. I hope this will help us move forward together. All I want is a future with Nina.

My father is MIA, and my mother has gone into hiding. God only knows where. So much for motherly love. Bitsy has been humiliated, so she's running away to lick her wounds. Melanie was originally orchestrating the reunion, but she, too, ran away to hide from the taunting public eye, so there were a lot of things undone. You see, Melanie isn't a delegator, so the reunion committee was losing their shit over what to do when she suddenly dropped off the face of the planet. The good news was the decorations were sort of in line with a prom theme. Marley, Cassie, Addie, and George jumped in to add a bit more magic to the space. I know, right? Stop it. I know you are so impressed with my grand romantic gesture. Nina didn't get the prom she deserved, but now she will.

I walk into the large dining room of the pretentious country club with a sense of awe. George called in a few favors from his designer friends, and the place has been transformed into a magical romantic scene. Candles flicker on the tables that are adorned with crisp, white linen. There is an expanded dance floor with an '80s cover band, simply because my girl loves '80s music. The bar is stocked and ready for business. I am pretty jazzed with how well this all came together so quickly. While money can't buy happiness, it can create a scene that invites that very feeling.

People start to trickle in, and the committee members distribute name tags. I greet some of them as they make their way to the bar. I make small talk, which I hate, but it helps ease my nerves. I've been more nervous in the time Nina and I have been trying to get it together than in my entire life. But when Addie and Jameson stopped by early to check in, Addie assured me that Nina would love this gesture, and Jameson just slapped me on the back. That's man-speak for "good job."

My eyes catch Nina as she steps into the venue. Her lips move as she silently reads the sign inside the entrance: "Prom Revisited." She bites her lower lip, probably as nervous as I am but for different reasons, and after a few words with Addie and a hug, her eyes search for me. I make my way toward her. She's a vision in a fitted, pink, silk cocktail dress, her black hair styled in a sophisticated twist. She looks like a goddess.

We stand face to face. Our lips inches from each other and her body flush with mine.

"Harrison, did you do this? You gave me the prom I missed." Tears escape her eyes.

I gently wipe away the tears and say, "I would do anything to take away the pain I caused you that night. First, I need to get you a cocktail and share some information that I just learned regarding Melanie."

She groans. "It must be bad if I need a cocktail." Her eyes narrow.

We head to the bar, order our drinks, and find a quiet place just outside the room.

Nina takes a long drink of her martini and says, "Okay, let's hear it."

"Melanie is pregnant, but I am not the father."

"Okay, that's great news, but I can tell there's more. Like, how did you find out this information without a paternity test and who is the actual father?"

"That's an interesting story. It seems that your fake spouse and Melanie were hooking up. Apparently, when Antonio was leaving a meeting with my father at his office, they happened to run into each other. They started seeing each other, which resulted in a pregnancy."

"I did not see that coming." She takes another long drink of her cocktail.

"I don't think anyone did. While Antonio was under surveillance, a woman was spotted visiting him quite frequently. With facial recognition technology, she was identified as Melanie. She's now MIA as well. The agents have a warrant since she did participate in aiding a known criminal. Since this is her first offense and her role was small, she might get off with a slap on the wrist."

"Anything else I need to know?"

"Well, I did want to tell you that I am in love with you and desperately want to be together. I want a future with you, Nina. No more excuses. Are you in this with me?" I whisper.

"I'm in. Let's see what all the fuss is about being in a relationship." She smirks.

At that very moment, the '80s cover band starts playing "Don't Stop Believing," and Nina grins. I grab her hand and we head to the dance floor. George is already dancing with Addie, who is screaming the lyrics at the top of her lungs. Jameson is nursing his bourbon, obviously amused by his fiancée, and Lillie coaxes a reluctant Mason onto the dance floor. I can't help but think how funny life is and that just when you think something isn't going to work out, it magically does—and even better than you could ever imagine.

Nina

I don't remember ever feeling so happy. If there's a possibility of floating on air, I'm claiming it. We enter Grammy's house to find my spunky grandmother making a lunch spread while being entertained by Owen and Maddie's dancing antics. Lillie and Mason are sitting next to each other with their hands intertwined. Could life be any better?

Grammy sees us and her face lights up. She grabs my hand and says, "You look happy."

"Grammy, I'm filled up." I grin at her. Any time I was struggling, she would tell me that you have to fill yourself up because you can't depend on other people to do it for you. Happiness is, after all, an inside job.

Harrison wraps his arms around me, and Grammy smiles as she reaches for Harrison's hand. She knew. She always knew that he was the one. I guess I just needed the universe to kick my ass.

Owen and Maddie are cracking up about some video they're watching on Lillie's tablet. I tilt my head a bit at Lillie and say, "So, how are things going?"

She blushes and Mason gives me his usual neutral appearance.

Lillie clears her throat, probably as a distraction method, and says, "Mason is moving to New York." Her cheeks pinken as she shares the news.

"That's amazing! Double—no, wait, *triple* dates are in our future! Mason, I will get to see you all the time." I'm elated that my cousin has found love and I get to see him more often. It's so foreign to see him like this. Comfortable and content.

My thoughts are interrupted when I hear Owen say to Harrison, "I can't believe your girlfriend is Nina. Now who will be my wingman?"

"Don't worry, buddy. Jameson and I will still help you with the ladies."

Owen looks at him with a disgusted expression. "I'm a player and you two are going to cramp my style with your women. Relationships are clock blockers."

Harrison glances at me and says, "Owen, it's cock block, and someday you'll find that perfect someone who will make you want to just be with them."

I swoon. Harrison smirks and Owen shakes his head like he can't believe another one bit the dust. There is definitely something in the water with all the coupledom.

EPILOGUE

Harrison

I wake up the next morning to Nina comfortably nestled in my arms. The sound of the ocean from our gorgeous room in Antigua adds to my contentment. My brain spans the unbelievable past few days, and I snuggle her a little bit closer. Contrary to what Addie thought, Nina and I actually really did rest when we got here. Nina passed out mid-kiss. We'll have plenty of time to "rest" for a long, long time.

The woman of the hour raises her head and squints at me.

"Morning, gorgeous." I grin.

"Ugh. What time is it?" she grunts.

"I forgot how delightful you are in the morning. It's around eight. I thought we would grab some breakfast. What time do you have to meet Addie at the spa?"

I lean over to kiss her. She promptly puts her hand in front of her mouth.

"No kissing until my breath is fresher."

I put up my hands in surrender as she stumbles out of bed and into the bathroom. I hop—no, really, I'm hopping because I'm *that* ecstatic—out of bed and call room service. I know how she is until she's fueled by the caffeine gods.

My phone rings and I see it's Jameson.

"Good morning! Happy wedding day!"

"Thank you. You sound exceedingly chipper this morning. Did you get plenty of rest?" Fucker starts to laugh.

"We seriously did get plenty of rest. She practically passed out on me."

"Can't say I blame her, since the past few weeks have been a bit eventful. Speaking of eventful, the FBI just arrested your father. My contact says they found him at an underground poker tournament dressed in drag. Fun fact, his stage name is Lovely Lyllia."

"I could have gone my whole life not knowing his drag name," I growl.

"I hear you, man. Also, I have a replacement investor for Nina. This guy is awesome, and he's always looking for new opportunities. He loves her story and is anxious to get on board. Total silent partner but happy to engage if asked."

"That's great news! Who is it?" I inquire. She's going to be so thrilled.

"It's me."

I pause. Of course it is. I can't believe this didn't occur to me before. "I should have known when you touted how *awesome* he is, as you normally don't speak highly of anyone." I laugh.

"Whatever. This way she has somebody in her corner she trusts, and it's a great investment."

"I think it'll be good too. You guys can hash out the details once we get home."

"Sounds good. We have a tee time for eleven, so that will give us time to shower and dress; the photographer wants us ready by five for photos. Owen says he is going to kick our asses, so bring your A game." He chuckles.

"Sounds good, man." There's a knock on the door. "Hey, room service is at the door with breakfast and coffee. My girl is a bit scary before coffee, so I'll catch you later at the golf course."

"See you then."

We disconnect our call. I open the door and take the cart as I give the guy a tip. Just as I settle the cart in the room, she appears from the bathroom. I present her with her cup of liquid gold and watch her demeanor change once it hits her bloodstream. It's like watching a mood ring fluctuate.

"Mmm ... that's the stuff."

I grab her and kiss the sass right out of her because, well, I can.

"Well, that was quite a greeting."

"We have wasted so much time, so I'm playing catch-up." I am grinning.

"You are adorable, and I'm happy to play catch-up anytime, but I need to get ready to meet Addie at the spa."

"We have plenty of time, plus I have news from Jameson. He called while you were brushing your teeth."

"How is the groom this morning? Is he nervous?"

"No, he seems excited. We're playing golf while you all do your spa thing. Owen says he's going to kick our asses." I chuckle.

"He probably will. Okay, tell me the news and it better be good because we're due for that."

She is right on the mark with that statement.

"I'm pleased to tell you that my dad was arrested while dressed in drag at an underground poker game." I put my hand up to stop her because I know she's going to want the details of his drag identity, and frankly, I don't want to discuss it. "The best news is that you have a new investor. He'll be a silent partner like you wanted, and he's awesome. His words, not mine." I laugh.

"I'm assuming that you don't want to discuss your father. That's fine. You know I'll get the details from Addie." She grins. "So, who is this *awesome* investor?"

"It's Jameson." I shrug.

"That's perfect!" she squeals. "Although his fiancée might be an issue. She's so opinionated and eats way too much chocolate." Her eyes glint with humor.

I laugh at her. My heart beats harder seeing her so carefree. Honestly, I have never seen her so relaxed. We're finally getting our chance and I couldn't be happier.

"Alright, Ms. Sassy. We have plenty of time to celebrate our good fortune before you leave for the spa." I wiggle my eyebrows.

"I like how you think."

We spend the next few hours playing catch-up.

Nina

"Stop eating that chocolate, Addie. It feels like it's 112 degrees, and you're going to get chocolate all over your Vera Wang gown." I berate her as if she were a small child, which she sometimes acts like.

"I can't help it! I'm about to get married and I'm nervous." She pops another piece.

"Why can't you be an adult and take a Xanax?" I ask.

"You know why I can't. That one time I did—at that book signing after my memoir was published—and I fell asleep."

Oh shit. How could I forget that gem of a moment?

"That was epic." I giggle.

"No, but it was a really good nap." She smirks.

George comes running in, shouting, "Five minutes!" and Addie stuffs another chocolate in her mouth.

I grab her hands, look her in the eye, and say, "You are loved—by me, by Owen, by all your friends, and by your almost-husband. Today is about the celebration of you and Jameson. Your love story was created because you stepped out of your comfort zone, and I played matchmaker." It's true … I did. She thought she would be getting a young, bubbly female publicist, but I had other ideas. My gut told me that they needed each other. I am *that* good.

Addie rolls her eyes. "Yes, Nina. You are the guru of matchmaking, which is why you resorted to a dating app that ended up matching you with the person you had been resisting for years."

"We aren't talking about me. This is your day. He adores you and Owen. I am so honored to be at your side. I love you, Addie."

"I love you, Nina."

"Jesus! You all are seconds from ruining the makeup that I worked too hard on for you all to mess up. Let's go!" George commands.

"You need to get laid," Addie quips.

We hustle down the hallway to the open French doors that lead to the beach. The sun is setting, with the walkway illuminated by candles. I make my way down the aisle. Jameson looks like he's going to hurl while Owen and Harrison are grinning from ear to ear. I wink and take my place awaiting the arrival of my beautiful bestie.

The biggest surprise was that she asked her father, Wendell Brooks, to walk her down the aisle. He has worked hard on repairing and building their relationship, so this was a big step in the healing process. She is beaming. Her strapless dress is a soft-crepe mermaid gown that accentuates her curvy figure. It's stunning on her. Her father's face is wet with tears. When she reaches Jameson, it's as if the world stops for just the two of them. So much adversity to get to this place, but they are here committing to each other.

I catch Harrison's eye. He mouths, "I love you," and I mouth back, "I love you more." This is just the beginning of our story, and I can't wait to experience every moment with him.

Acknowledgments

To my incredible family and tribe of soul sisters thank you for believing in me. Your unwavering support empowers me to be the best version of myself. The most exquisite part of life is knowing you never have to do anything alone.

To my amazing editor, Christie Stratos of Proof Positive, thank you for your incredible feedback. Your encouragement has been a huge catalyst in this journey.

Finally, thank you to those who have chosen to read my written words. I hope that these characters find a place in your heart like they have mine.